WINTER WONDERLANDS

TEN TALES OF HOLIDAY MAGIC

DAYLE A. DERMATIS

About This Book

Accidentally summoning a Solstice deity.

Dealing with a magically super-annoying HOA.

Visiting a haunted Adirondack inn on Christmas Eve.

What, don't things like this happen to everyone during the holidays?

If not, experience them vicariously! Snuggle before a roaring fire with a beverage of your choice and enjoy these ten tales of winter holiday magic, mystery, and romance.

~

"[Desperate Housewitches] is wonderful, funny, and a do-not-miss."

– Kristine Kathryn Rusch
Hugo-award winning author

CONTENTS

WINTER WONDERLANDS

LAST CHRISTMAS

I was finally alone in the ski chalet, my feet propped up on the coffee table in front of the fire, a cup of cocoa with a generous splash of crème de menthe cradled in my hands, when the ghosts walked in.

I heard the front door open and a voice I didn't recognize chirp, "Omigod!" at which point I reacted much like a sleeping cat who suddenly feels the cold, wet nose of a curious greyhound in its butt.

In other words, I shot out of my comfortable chair and spun around. "Who the hell are you?"

"Who the hell are *you*?" When she said this, in an English accent, she flipped her head sideways, but not a single strand of her back-combed, teased, hairsprayed expanse of blond hair moved. A hurricane wouldn't have caused a single strand to stir. "We reserve this lodge every year."

Her puffy ski jacket was hot pink with turquoise diagonal stripes on the front, and her ski pants were the same color with pink piping. Her fingernails were painted a virulent lime green not found in nature (thank goodness), and her eyeshadow matched the turquoise of her spiral earrings and her outfit.

No, she didn't have bad fashion taste—at least not according to her era. My tingly ability to recognize a ghost served me well. The other way to identify a ghost is if they touch you. You know when the *Titanic* hits the iceberg? You feel like you've been subsumed by the iceberg.

She dropped her duffel bag just inside and kicked her enormous boots against the side of the doorway to dislodge the snow, then stepped in, followed by another woman and two men wearing similar bright clothes.

Her glossy pink lips dipped in a frown. "Why is it so different in here? What happened?"

I bit my lip. "Umm..."

The reason I hadn't encountered a ghost on our annual Christmas trip to this Alpine resort was because we'd never stayed in this chalet before.

Usually we stay in a much bigger chalet, flying in relatives from all corners of the world, but this year's heavy snowstorms meant the rest of our clan couldn't make it due weather-cancelled flights. The hotel offered us the option of switching to a smaller, newly renovated, ultra-luxury chalet that was farther up the mountain from the main building.

Yes, my family is rich enough to fly in cousins and aunts and uncles from everywhere and cover an all-expenses-paid vacation at a swanky ski lodge. After all, my father is Edward Ashburne, one of the best known and successful producers in the business.

And yes, that makes me Nikki Ashburne, former Hollywood party girl until my fall from grace.

When my beloved grandmother died, I went to from her funeral to a party where for the first time I popped some pills along with several drinks, and like an idiot, I OD'd and briefly died.

When I woke up in the hospital, my grandmother—the aforementioned deceased one—was sitting on the edge of my bed. She slapped me and told me I was stupid, and then disappeared.

I assumed it was a one-shot experience except, during my time at the rehab-cum-spa I hid out in afterwards, I met another ghost, a young woman from the 1970s who'd decided the spa was a safe place to stay rather than moving on.

In my experience, ghosts generally stick around not because of revenge or unfinished business, but because they were happy in their life and didn't feel the pull of loved ones who'd preceded them. I've occasionally had a ghost pop up to ask for a favor of a living loved one, but never in a negative way.

Clearly these four felt their annual holiday jaunt was super-important.

"The resort remodeled it," I said. They had all entered and were staring at me as if I were the ghost. "My family and I usually stay in a different chalet, but they gave us this one this year."

"Well, that is just bogus," one of the men said, rather bitterly.

"Yeah," the first woman said. "*We* reserve this chalet every year. Just cause they remodeled...."

"Are you sure you reserved it?" I asked.

Her shoulders rose as she shook her head dismissively. "*I'm* not in charge of that. Lynda always handled it." She said the last in a tone of voice that implied organization was beneath her.

All four of them turned and looked at each other, understanding dawning on their faces.

I took a long swallow of my laced cocoa. It was starting to cool, but it still tasted good. "Let me guess," I said. "Lynda is no longer with you?"

They shook their heads.

"Have a seat," I said. "This might take some time."

I really hoped they knew they were dead. That's a beyond awkward conversation. Often they don't take the news well.

They sat on a sofa and I took a comfy chair across from them.

When I said I'd been alone before the group arrived, I fibbed. Maggie, a four-year-old with blond curls, was my constant companion. She doesn't speak, for reasons I have yet to learn. She plopped cross-legged on the floor next to my chair.

Hopefully, my parents and my brother wouldn't come back anytime soon.

After a morning of snowboarding, my brother, Ned, went down to the main lodge probably to hit up some girls and/or see if there were any music producers vacationing who might be interested in his band's music. Even though Ned barely speaks to me because he thinks I'm lying about seeing ghosts, neither of us are stupid enough to go snowboarding alone. No matter what, in the end we had each other's backs.

My mother was in the main lodge probably schmoozing and showing off her new winter wardrobe. My father had gone down to use the resort's private business office.

I introduced myself, and the four ghosts did the same.

Brandy was the blond. Next to her was Cy, who had feathered brown hair and puppy-dog brown eyes. Then

Paul, a handsome black man, and Marcella, who had short, curly dark hair cut in a wedge. All of them were fit, and pretty (yes, even the men), even with the bright makeup and big hair. (I wasn't really judging. Hey, I remember when fashion trends were vitally important to me.)

All of their accents were some flavor of British. Different, but I couldn't say who was from where, and it really didn't matter. They all sounded fairly posh, which made sense, since they had to have had money to rent a chalet every year for the holidays, even a small, formerly simple one.

Marcella reached into an inside pocket of her white puffy coat and leaned across the coffee table to hand me a Polaroid photo. I took it carefully, making sure not to touch her and watch my fingers turn to ice and shatter. (I don't think that could happen. But best to be safe.)

The photo was of a group of people, including the four sitting across from me, in a living room with plain, boxy wooden columns, and brown curtains, and mismatched furniture. Maybe they'd turned the lights down for atmosphere, but it looked depressingly dark.

Yep, that one-story living room looked nothing like this place.

Now, the two-story vaulted great room with one wall of windows filled the chalet with light. A second-floor balcony ringed the room on three sides and led to the bedrooms, each of which had its own fireplace. Caramel-colored, polished log walls gleamed. The furniture was "rustic" insofar that it was made out of logs, but the sofas and chairs were comfortable, and the beds had high-end mattresses and bedding.

There was twice-daily maid service, and chef-prepared meals delivered for lunch and dinner (for breakfast, we made do with a Slayer Espresso Machine and fresh pastries, bagels, and fruit, or we could make our own from the fully stocked fridge and pantry). Right now, the place smelled like pine and wood smoke and the clam chowder and fresh-baked rosemary bread we'd had for lunch along with a crudités plate with three kinds of homemade dips, and dessert.

A two-story spruce tree was tastefully decorated with multicolored lights and clear glass soap-bubble-like ornaments that reflected the red, blue, green, and yellow. The resort had hung stockings with our names on them over the fireplace.

I set the photo back on the coffee table. Something about it bothered me, but I couldn't put my mental finger on it.

"How can you *see* us?" Paul asked.

I blew out a relieved breath and gulped more cocoa. At least I didn't have to explain that they were life-challenged. "I don't know how—I just do," I said. "I've never met anybody else who can."

Brandy had been quiet up until now. She sighed dramatically.

"Right, here's the deal: we come up here every year," she said. "We always book this cabin. You'll have to leave."

"Yeah, no, I don't think so," I said. "For one thing, my family and I are still alive, so I think we take precedence."

Cy nudged her with his elbow, kinda hard, making no effort to hide the action. She shot him a grumpy glance and he whispered something in her ear. She whispered back. I couldn't hear what they were saying, but it sounded like an argument.

Finally Brandy huffed and sat back.

"You're right," she said. "You get precedence." But then

her lower lip started to quiver, and I thought, *Oh crap, here we go.*

"It's just...we were always so happy here." She sniffed, a bit dramatically. I couldn't tell if her nose was red because she was about to burst into tears or from the cold outside, but then I wondered if ghosts felt cold and heat. I bit my tongue to keep from asking.

"Mostly," someone murmured, so quiet I almost missed it. Cy, I thought. The quick snort came from Marcella.

I leaned back in my chair and blew out a breath, running my hands through my unfashionable but adorable (if I do say so myself) 1920s shoulder-length bob. I wished I had more cocoa. Or just crème de menthe. Or, ideally, a nice peaty whiskey.

We did have some lovely whiskey, but not right now.

Ghosts could become more corporeal when they wanted to, and hold on to things they hadn't had with them when they died. (They keep their clothes, etc., and can't change them.) If I got myself a drink, I'd have to be polite and offer to get them something, too, and if Daddy's whiskey disappeared too fast, there'd be hell to pay. (At least until he got the resort to fly another one in for him.)

"There's been crappy weather all over the place, and a lot of people had to cancel their reservations," I said. "I'm sure tons of other chalets are empty. You could go to one of those."

"But *this* was *our place!*" Brandy wailed.

Paul leaned forward to see her. "It could work, luv. This one's so different now anyway."

She scowled at him. "It doesn't matter."

Hoo boy. Drama queen much? The others looked a little uncomfortable at her insistence, but for whatever reason, they weren't arguing with her. Probably so they didn't have to listen to this for the entirety of their stay.

The chalet had five bedrooms, all en suite. The primary bedroom my parents shared, Ned's and my rooms, one that my dad was using as a makeshift office, and the one my mother was using as a closet and dressing room (although how she could need that many clothes for a week-long trip is baffling.)

"You guys know how to filter, right?" I asked.

Four blank stares.

"Maybe you call it something different," I said. "You can…go to that in-between place?"

Again, this was something I didn't entirely understand. Ghosts can wink out and reappear anywhere else, but there was also some nether region type of thing they could stay in.

"Ah," Paul said as the others nodded. "Yes, we can."

"Here's what I'm thinking," I said. "My parents and my brother—and I assume the staff—have no idea about ghosts. I don't want them running into any of you or vice versa, in terms of freezing their asses off. If my mother thinks there's a draft in here, she'll raise enough of a stink that someone will get fired. Okay so far?"

"I'm cool," Cy said.

"Sure," Marcella said.

Paul nodded, and Brandy finally followed suit. She clearly didn't like rules or limitations—unless they were to her benefit.

"I can't talk to you while other people are in the room," I went on. "Don't try to engage me." Otherwise, my father would be concerned for me, my mother would either think I was on drugs (as if) or I needed to be committed, and Ned would get even more pissed off at me.

Once I got their okays there, I continued. "We're sleeping in three of the five bedrooms. The other two, my father and mother are using, but not at night. So you guys can sleep there."

If you sleep. Geez, I needed to start making a list of questions to ask some of my ghost friends back in California.

I was unprepared for the glances that shot between them, a combination of first surprise, then question and concern.

"What kind of beds are in the rooms?" Cy asked, his brow furrowed.

"Kings," I said.

"Some of us might prefer...separate accommodations," he said.

Brandy's expression shot daggers at him.

"That's all we've got," I said. "Take it or leave it. Stay or filter and go away." I leaned forward, elbows on my knees. "Look, I'm trying to figure out a way to make this work, but we've got to compromise."

"No problem here," Marcella said, and Paul nodded.

Cy and Brandy exchanged another look and acquiesced.

Outside, I heard voices. Crap.

"Grab your stuff just in case, and get up there or out of here," I said. "Stow your stuff in the office closet. Give me time to process with my family around."

I thought longingly to the time when I'd been alone, just a couple hours earlier.

Why does my ability to see ghosts—and my knee-jerk reaction to help them—have to be so complicated?

~

Our uninvited guests behaved themselves for the evening. The staff always sets the entire massive dining room table, which seats twelve, with white plates atop gold chargers and multiple gold-rimmed wine glasses. The four were able to avoid sitting immediately next to any of us. Where their food came from, I have no idea, but clearly nobody else saw them eating and drinking, or carrying on a separate conversation.

It was confusing, but I survived.

After everyone went to bed, I found it hard to sleep, so I grabbed my Kindle and went back down to curl up under a blanket on a comfy chair and read. The fire was mostly just coals and a few flickers of flame, but I could still feel its warmth.

Turned out there was one other person who was having trouble sleeping: Paul. I went to the bar for a glass of wine and asked him if he wanted anything.

"Rum and Coke if you've got it."

Of all of them, Paul seemed the most grounded, chill, although Marcella seemed okay, too. Cy seemed nice, but my guess was that he got by on his pretty-boy looks more than anything else.

We chatted for a few moments, then he asked, "Why have you not asked what happened to us?"

I swirled the amber liquid in my glass. "I don't think it's polite. If a ghost wants to tell me, great, but otherwise it's none of my business."

He smiled, his teeth white against the darkness of his skin. "That *is* terribly polite of you," he said. "And I don't mind a bit."

There had been ten of them in the past, although a couple of people shifted over the four years they'd come here. When they left the last time, in 1987, the group had been separated into two gondola cars for the trip down the mountain.

Something went wrong with main cable for this group's car....

He didn't need to elaborate. Thankfully.

This had happened a good thirty-plus years ago—well before I entered the world—but still, I was amazed that the resort had been able to downplay the accident and stay afloat. Europeans weren't as sue-happy as Americans, but still. Or maybe the resort's owners had abandoned ship and a new group was in charge by now.

Anyway, the surviving members brought a few more friends and kept the tradition going for a few years, but it wasn't the same, and finally they decided to avoid the bad memories and go somewhere else for the holidays. Brandy, Cy, Paul, and Marcella had of course come back every year with their friends, and even after their friends stopped, they continued.

"Force of habit, I guess," Paul said with a quick laugh.

I wondered what it would be like to have friends like that, friends you happily went on vacation with every year. I thought I'd had a great group of close friends before my unfortunate error in judgment, but I'd been wrong. They'd all turned away.

After that, I realized they'd been kind of shitty friends all along.

Now all of my friends were ghosts. Harder to go on vacation with them, unless it's remote enough that nobody's around to worry about me talking to myself all the time.

"That still sucks," I said.

"I choose not to fight against things I can't change," he said.

We finished our drinks, and the wine had done its work on me. The big gooshy bed with the million pillows and warm flannel sheets sounded heavenly. (Oops. Haha.)

I took our glasses to the sink, and said goodnight. Paul slowly faded away. I assumed he was going to bed and didn't feel like taking the stairs.

I was in bed and almost asleep when I realized what bothered me about the Polaroid Marcella had showed me of the good ol' days.

Now, Brandy and Cy were together, as were Paul and Marcella.

But in the photo, Brandy had been curled on a beanbag chair with Paul, and Marcella had been sitting on the arm of Cy's chair.

Maybe *that* was what was keeping them coming back?

I'd gotten complacent when dinner and the rest of the evening had gone smoothly. The next morning, Ned complained grumpily about me running my blow dryer too early in the morning, and then doing it *again*.

I hadn't even showered yet; I'd been planning to do that after snowboarding today. Out of the corner of my eye, Marcella shook her head, indicating it hadn't been her.

Brandy didn't bother too look ashamed. I took her aside later and asked why she'd needed to dry her hair, much less *twice*, and she widened her eyes innocently and said, "Because it didn't come out right the first time."

I didn't have the heart to tell her that not only was she stuck in her clothes, she was stuck with her hair. It was never going to change. She didn't need to do anything to it.

My eagle-eyed father noticed the amount in his

whiskey bottle was a bit lower than he'd expected, but he wasn't outright angry. He just gave Ned and I a small scowl, and a moment later he was ruffling my hair and laughing about something else.

It was Christmas Eve, and after dinner, Brandy tried to rope me into their argument about when they should open presents. Even though I ignored her, she wouldn't stop, so I finally made a shooing motion with my hand.

"Everything all right, dear?" my mother asked.

Crap. Of course she'd notice.

"Thought I saw a bug," I said. "It was just a piece of tinsel." Then I excused myself to use the bathroom, and Brandy followed me just as I expected her to, because she wasn't through making me see her point of view yet.

I reminded her about the no-engaging-me-when-others-are-around rule, and suggested they open their presents tonight, so they didn't accidentally brush up against the rest of us on Christmas morning.

Apparently that had been her argument all along, because she smiled and left.

Thank goodness. I could pee in peace.

~

THAT NIGHT, Ned went down to the main lodge and my parents called it an early night; Daddy had a script to review and my mother had a stylist and makeup person coming in the morning because we were going to have family pictures taken.

Nothing says casual holiday photos like being perfectly coiffed and made up. The scent of her Chanel would overpower the pine and woodsmoke. She'd probably make me suffer the same fate, although I wouldn't let the stylist bully me into straightening my hair, dammit. Never again. I loved my curls, fashion be damned.

Marcella put on her puffy white coat, a pack of cigarettes in her hand. I'd already asked them not to smoke inside, and although they occasionally forgot and lit up before remembering, they'd been good about it.

"Mind if I join you?" I asked.

"Sure, c'mon."

I pulled my own coat and boots out of the closet and put them on over my flannel jammies, which were blue with white snowflakes on them.

Marcella leaned on the quaint split-rail fence that surrounded the chalet, staring out at the snow-covered mountains. Even at night, they had a faint glow. Light briefly flared across her face when she lit her cigarette. She didn't offer me one, because I'd already said I didn't smoke.

"Beautiful here," I said. "I wouldn't like to live in the cold, but for a week, it's perfect."

"Yeah," she said. "It's bril. We always had a laugh up here, even if it was a bit of a shambles sometimes." She glanced at me, saw the look on my face, and laughed. "Sorry, forgot you were a Yank. A bit of a mess."

"Romantically?"

She toasted me with her cigarette. "Got it in one. Put a group of people in a cabin for a week and sometimes it can get a bit tight." She tapped out her cigarette. "Me and Cy came up here together, and that's when I met Paul. Cy's a great guy, really, but he's kind of dim. Good for a laugh, but that's it. Paul's more, I don't know, thoughtful?"

"Smart?"

"That, yeah, and deeper, I guess. Anyway, Cy didn't take it well. The next year, he brought Brandy. I'm not sure if he loves her or if he's trying to show I'm replaceable." She tapped ash into the snow. "I've been thinking about bouncing, but I really do care for Paul, you know? And if I decide not to come back here..." She shrugged. "What if that means I'm accepting..." she waved her hand "...whatever's out there?"

"Have you talked to Paul about it?"

She took a drag on her cigarette, blew the smoke out on a sigh. "No. Kind of haven't worked up the courage yet."

"He might surprise you."

"He might at that." She flicked her butt over the fence. I winced. Hopefully nobody else could see it but me. "Thanks, Yank. See you inside."

I enjoyed the muffled silence that snow provides and the stars glittering bright without all the light pollution in LA.

Then I heard footsteps crunching in the snow up the path to the shuttle from the lodge.

"What are you doing out there?" Ned asked. I smelled alcohol on his breath, but he was tipsy, not drunk and slurring.

"Pondering the mysteries of life," I said.

"You weren't...?"

I held up a hand. "Don't be asking questions you don't want to hear the answers too, baby brother."

He frowned. "Right. Jaysus, Nikki."

"It really is beautiful out," I said. "Come and look at the stars with me?"

"Nah," he said. "I'm gonna have a nightcap and crash."

"Sounds like a good plan. I'll join you."

He didn't look excited by the prospect, but he didn't push me away, either. We briefly made plans to snowboard in the afternoon since morning would be family time, but otherwise we didn't really talk. Still, it was better than nothing. It's not like I'd been expecting a Christmas miracle.

PRESENTS HAD BEEN OPENED and casual staged photographed had been taken (my mother was cranky about my hair, but I think she knew it was a fight she'd lost long ago), soon to appear in some select, snooty magazines. Now my father was taking a nap, my mother was in the bath, and Ned was showering post-snowboarding.

When Ned and I had walked in, I knew there was trouble in paradise. The ghosts were dressed in their snow gear, duffels at their feet. Marcella and Paul had strained looks on their faces. Cy looked sad and a little confused. Brandy was *clearly* unhappy.

So I stayed downstairs, making myself another cocoa with lots of crème de menthe. I'd hit the harder stuff if I needed to.

"Paul and Marcella are *leaving*," Brandy told me, pouting. "I mean, like, *permanently*. Can't you do something?"

Why she thought I was suddenly in charge of fixing everything was beyond me.

"They have the right to do what's best for them," I said. "It's their choice."

"But our holiday! We come here *every year*."

"Why?" I asked. "Why *do* you insist on coming back every year?" I asked.

"Because...because..." Her gaze darted around the room, finally resting on Paul's face before her lashes lowered.

"I keep telling you, it's not going to happen," he said. "I'm sorry, but no."

Tears glittered on her lashes now, and she sniffed.

Cy stared at her, disappointment in his eyes.

"But, but, where's the fun of *leaving*?" Brandy asked.

"You can see your family, other friends who've moved on. You might even find somebody new there."

She nodded slowly as she took this idea in. Suddenly, she gasped.

"Oooh! I might meet John Lennon!"

"Yes," I said wearily. How had they put up with her for so long? Three days and she'd already sucked the strength out of me. "I don't know how works, but it might actually be possible for you to meet John Lennon."

"Well, bugger it," Cy said, his own pretty face frowning. "What about me? Don't I get a say in this?"

"You can make your own choices too," I said, feeling much older than him. "You and Brandy can stay here, or you can move on. Those are the options everyone gets when they die."

"You can talk about it on the hike down," Paul suggested.

Upstairs, I heard Ned bellowing a holiday song. He was out of the shower.

Paul got Brandy and Cy moving. Marcella, the last one out the door, turned back.

"Thanks again, Yank. Happy Christmas."

I waved. "Merry Christmas."

Then I sat down with my cocoa and closed my eyes. I wouldn't be alone for long, but I could savor the moment.

GOOD SCRYING GONE BAD

The first rule of witchcraft is the one everyone knows: Harm none.

The second rule of witchcraft should be just as obvious: Practice magic only when you're clear of mind.

In my defense, I didn't realize we were practicing actual magic.

My cousin Carly and I were cleaning out our grandmother's house. Grandma Belinda had had her three-story split-level ranch custom-built in the seventies, so although it was reasonably tidy, it was still full of stuff. Every closet, every bureau, every secret room was crammed with decades of memorabilia and tchotchkes and magical paraphernalia—sometimes it was hard to tell those apart— outdated clothing, and more blockbuster paperbacks from the eighties than you could imagine anyone could read in a lifetime.

"All the important things I care about are in storage," Grandma Belinda had said when she charged us with the task.

"What do you want us to do with all of this?" Carly has asked.

"Whatever," Grandma Belinda said carelessly, waving her vape cigarette in an expansive gesture. Imagine a cross between Joan Collins and Shirley Maclaine, but someone who could actually turn you into a newt, and you get the picture. "Take what you want, sell the rest, or, hell, light a match and walk away. I don't give a shit, really."

Then she hugged us in a cloud of White Shoulders, kissed each of our foreheads with a resounding smack that left a coral-pink lipstick print, and vanished with a faint *pop*.

Grandma Belinda was allegedly off on a cruise to Tahiti. Carly and I weren't sure if she really was on a cruise to Tahiti or if that was a euphemism for something. Getting plastic surgery done, maybe, or going through a reincarnation.

It was the end of the first day, and we were making good use of Grandma Belinda's liquor cabinet. The collection of bottles had been dusty, but it was top shelf stuff, and I had made some wicked Amaretto Sours. I made a mental note to find the recipe for a hangover banishing brew before we went to bed.

I felt grimy all the way down to my teeth. A shower sounded blissful. Grandma Belinda had smoked most of her life (hence the vapes: her most recent attempt to quit) and even though she'd spelled the smoke away, the odor still clung, faintly, deep down, in her things. I ached in muscles I hadn't previously been aware of, and I felt fifty instead of twenty-seven.

I was half-sprawled on a comfortable but hideous blue-with-white-flowers sofa in the den, and Carly was lying on the floor. She'd taken out the scrunchie she'd used to maintain her ponytail, and her blond hair fanned out across the large burgundy velour pillow she had propped against the brick hearth of the fireplace. We were the same age, and had been friends since we could cast spells between our cribs. She was trying to read a Harold Robbins novel out loud, but she kept dissolving into giggles every other sentence. The alcohol was either helping or hindering...it was hard to tell.

So far, we'd thrown out expired toiletries and makeup and potions, and everything in the fridge except for a few things we'd brought (Grandma Belinda wasn't much for cooking). We'd done a cursory sort through every room we could find, and discussed what size dumpster we'd need to order. (Nobody wanted home-taped entire series of *Bewitched* and *Charmed*, we were pretty sure.)

I sat up straighter to mix us each another drink on the blond wood coffee table.

"To us," I said, handing Carly her glass.

"To us," she agreed, "because we kick butt."

"My butt feels pretty kicked, actually," I said, groaning as I leaned back. I took a hefty swallow of my drink. Oh, yeah. "And I'm a little dishappointed we haven't found anything salacious. I had my money on Grandma Belinda having a stash of *something*."

"Me too," Carly said. "I was just afraid it was going to be homemade porn."

Our grandfather had died years ago, and Grandma Belinda had been far from celibate in the intervening years. Good for her. But Carly was also right. I stopped any mental pictures before they could form in my brain.

Carly, after sipping more of her drink, set it and the Robbins novel on the coffee table and crawled over to a bulging bookcase we hadn't gone through yet.

"Hey, look, wasn't this ours?" She tossed a coloring book over her shoulder. It landed on the coffee table, almost knocking her drink off. I picked it up and opened it. "Mythical" beasts.

"Yep—I remember doing this rainbow hippogriff. You told me hippogriffs were only tawny yellow. You never had any respect for my art." I sniffed.

She wasn't listening, of course, and I wasn't really miffed, of course (although I was proud of my twenty-years' younger self's commitment to creatively ignoring the lines). She was still pulling out books.

"Check this out," she said, crawling back over to her pillow.

She held a small, saddle-stapled pamphlet with a shiny lavender cardstock cover, clearly decades old and only semiprofessionally produced. On the cover, surrounded by hearts and cupids, were the words *How to Find Your One True Love Through Magic*.

It was probably a gag gift. We witches do that to one another. Astrology scrolls, fluffy New Age books written by people calling themselves Pixie Moonshadow, ceramic jars that say Eye of Newt, that sort of thing.

Without taking her eyes from the book, Carly reached out, picked up her drink, took a hefty swallow, and set the glass down again. "Madison, OMG, we have to do this!"

"What?" I wasn't sure what could top Harold Robbins.

"Okay, it says if you walk upstairs backwards holding a mirror and a candle, you'll see the face of your future husband gazing back at you."

"That's ridiculous," I said. "The future isn't set—"

"Oh, don't be such a party pooper. It'll be fun. It's just silly."

"Okay, you're on." I remembered a silver-backed, or

maybe silver-plated-backed, mirror in one of the bathrooms, and unsteadily made my wobbly way there. After I peed—why pass up the opportunity, since I was already there?—I grabbed it and went back to the den.

In the meantime, Carly had produced a white taper candle in a crystal candlestick. Because if there's anything a witch's house isn't lacking, it's candles.

"I'll go first," she said. She pointed a finger at the candle and a flame sizzled and flared, then she took the mirror from me. She made her way, a bit unsteadily, to the staircase that led up out of the den, and positioned herself at the foot, facing away. The open stairs were covered with turquoise carpet and flanked by a wrought-iron bannister.

Her hair was sticking out, she had a smudge of dirt on her face, and her cute tortoiseshell glasses were askew. I wondered how she could see straight, alcohol or not.

"Okay," she said. "Now turn out all the lights."

"What?"

"It said you have to do this in a dark house. Otherwise what would the candle be for? Sheez."

That made sense, at least to my very tipsy brain. I flipped down two switches, then clicked the dimmer switch.

There was some light on upstairs somewhere, but it was just a faint glow at the top of the stairs, around the corner after the landing and the second flight. It was dark enough for Carly, though.

She giggled as she felt for the first stair with her foot, stepped up, then fumbled for the next. "This is hard."

"If you fall and break your neck, don't come haunting to me," I said, but I was laughing, too.

When she got to the landing, I turned the lights back

on. She shifted the mirror to the hand holding the candle, and gripped the railing on the way down.

"Well?" I asked.

"If that was my future husband, he looks shushpiciously like me," she said. "And he needs a haircut."

I snorted. "Give me those." I took the mirror and candle, got into position, and waited for her to turn off the lights.

"Hecate's ass, you're right—this isn't easy." I made it up the first step before I held the mirror up. I barely could see a wavery shadow of the side of my face illuminated by the small candle flame. I giggled and wobbled my way up another few steps, and then—

—and then someone else stared out of the mirror at me.

Blond hair. Eyes the color of sea glass. Grecian nose.

And looking terrified.

He mouthed something that looked an awful lot like "Help me," before I tripped on the last step and fell backwards onto the landing. The candle and mirror went flying.

What. The. Fairies?

GRANDMA BELINDA's offhand comment about torching the place almost became prophetic, but Carly was sober enough to put out the burning carpet before the flames spread. I would've helped, but I was scrambling around looking for the mirror.

When I picked it up, I heard the crunch and tinkle of glass falling.

The mirror had busted, but good. There weren't even enough shards left to show the fractured pieces of my mystery man's face if I could figure out how to bring it back.

"What *happened?*" Carly demanded.

I told her.

"So you got to see your future husband and I didn't?" Carly stuck out her lower lip.

I knew she was joking, but I was still a little freaked out. "He is *not* my future husband!" I said. "He's clearly someone who needs help. I hope that mirror wasn't the only conduit he can use."

I walked backwards up the stairs with every other mirror in the house that wasn't nailed to a wall and that I could hold in one hand (Carly stood close by with a bowl of water in case I flung the candle again), but I didn't see anything but my blurry face. I looked in the rest of the mirrors, too, just in case, clutching the candle.

I knew better than to try an actual spell, given the state we were in. Eventually we admitted defeat, had another drink—while discussing increasingly far-fetched possibilities of what to do and who he might be—and went to bed.

Of course I forgot to find the recipe for hangover banishing brew, so I had to dig it out the next morning, and *that* was un-fun.

With clearer heads, we decided research was in order. So we did the next obvious thing: we called our mothers.

Neither had any experience or knowledge about this kind of phenomenon, although my mother said the man might be connected to me somehow already, even though I didn't recognize him. Both said they'd pass the question along.

We tried contacting Grandma Belinda, but all we got was a postcard fluttering through the air. One side showed a picture of a glittering white-sand beach, turquoise water lapping at the edge. The other side said "Wish you were here, except that you're busy cleaning out the house. Toodles!"

That still didn't really answer the question of where she truly was, even, since she'd obviously spelled it ahead of time to arrive at that moment.

We didn't find anything else in Grandma Belinda's house that spoke to the problem of who the man was (I'd hoped for a photo album, maybe), how I'd connected with him or made it possible for him to connect with me, or how to do it again, or anything. But we did find the missing and long-sought-after Amulet of Ra-Hep (the Magical Council was going to blow a gasket over that), Grandma Belinda's pet basilisk (contentedly living off a case of Cheetos in the sewing room), a possible doorway to Hell (we wisely left it chained shut), and a videotape of what might well have been homemade porn (which we destroyed with magical fire, although we considered tossing it through the possible doorway to Hell).

By Sunday evening, we were knackered, and I was no closer to figuring out who my mystery man was. It would take several more weekends to finish cleaning out the place, so we closed up the house and headed to our respective homes.

Monday I was back to work. I was a designer at a publisher of grimoires, spellbooks, and magic literature. What? We don't all run magic shops or psychic reading services.

The weather had turned from late summer haze to early autumn gentle rain. Raindrops ran down my office window, obscuring my view of the park across the street. Condensation gathered on the inside of the window from the heat off my computer and probably my own breath.

I had been intent on the copy placement on an ad for an upcoming release, so I didn't see the words written on the window right away.

The words were written backwards, as if the writer were standing outside.

My office is on the seventh floor.

And technically the words were on the inside, in the condensation, even though I was the only one there.

It said, *Who are you?*

I knew it was *him*. The mystery man from the mirror.

My head buzzing, I attempted to answer by writing backwards, to make it easier for him to read. *Madison Palles,* I painstakingly spelled out. *Who are you?*

I bit my lip, waiting for the response.

Then, slowly, *Brody*. The letters were front ways now, in the right direction. The last name was hard to read, though. Maybe it started with a W, or was than an H? *Can u help me?*

Given the obvious difficulty he was having writing, I forgave him the text speak. In fact, I used it myself, for expediency's sake.

I'll try. How? Where RU?

But the rain had stopped, and now sun pushed through the clouds, backlighting my window, and the condensation faded. If he responded, I couldn't see it.

~

LIKE A LOVESICK TEENAGER, I sketched him. My artistic skills were better than what my childhood coloring books suggested they'd be. For book covers, I mostly used a computer, but I had a decent hand.

First in pencil, then pen, and then I dug out my box of pastels, trying to capture those sea glass blue eyes. Any detail I could remember, before it was lost in memory.

I circulated the best sketch through the magical community as if I were looking for my lost familiar. *Have you seen Brody?* But nobody seemed to recognize him, or the name.

In my spare time, I researched scrying. Special mirrors, sacred pools, the shimmer of glowing coals, even crystal balls could all be conduits. Often it was used to see the future, even though that was one thing we witches couldn't really do, because the future is fluid. Then there was the whole "Mirror mirror on the wall" issue of who was really responding?

I didn't get any sense of malevolence from Brody. He seemed genuinely distressed.

Although, I admit, my sketches of him didn't show that terror in his eyes. If I thought too hard about that, I'd have nightmares.

If Brody was going to visit me in my dreams, I'd rather have them be helpful and constructive, if not actually pleasant.

But I still knew I needed to find a way to help him.

THE ANNUAL WINTER Solstice ritual was held every year on the Charles family estate, and was open to any witches worldwide who wanted to attend. I was never sure exactly how many people came, and suspected there was some kind of space vortex manipulation something or other going on, because the manor and gardens—palatial and expansive as they were, respectively—never seemed crowded.

The formal gardens on the longest night of the year was one of my favorite places. There's magic everywhere in the world (if you know how to see it), but some places just seem more magical than the rest. As if they're made of magic.

Maybe the magic is already there, or maybe we've imbued it with magic over centuries of rituals.

Or maybe I just love a ghostly formal garden in the dead of winter after midnight.

We'd completed the ritual for this year, and the sun would return. I mean, of course it would; that's basic science. We didn't control it, we just welcomed it. (Unless there's some inner circle with knowledge I'm not aware of. The Magical Council keeps pretty mum about a lot of things.) Still, I lingered in the garden.

The moon was fat and full, spreading silver light across the earth. The snow glowed as if it had its own source of light, and blanketed the world with silence, muffling even my breathing. It covered the hedge maze and the knot garden and the stone walls separating the different parts of the garden, and hugged the pergolas and gazebos. Everything was white and black, the color leached out of the world.

I was thinking about Brody and yet not thinking about him. My subconscious worked on the questions, the problem, all the time, but he wasn't in my direct thoughts. I know I wasn't thinking about scrying mediums, not even when I stopped by a marble birdbath.

The bowl was clear of snow, and a layer of ice covered the surface. The water and the ice on top were so black, they didn't even seem to reflect the moon...

As I watched, a hand pressed flat against the underside of the ice.

I didn't think. I only acted.

I made a fist and punched through the ice. Even

through my leather glove I could tell the water was bone-chillingly cold.

Magic works best without barriers. I pulled out, tugged off my glove, and plunged my bare hand into the birdbath.

The hand that met mine not only felt warm, it felt dry.

I wasn't sure what I was supposed to do. I couldn't exactly haul him out, or through, or whatever, because the circumference of the birdbath wasn't big enough for a man to fit through. In hindsight, that also prevented him from pulling *me* through.

In my defense...nope, I had no defense. It was probably a stupid thing to do. Carly was not the only one who'd pointed out to me that Brody might not be what he seemed. As in, he might be someone dangerous who had been deliberately and carefully imprisoned. He might have been put there—wherever *there* was, an alternate universe or a prison or just halfway across the world—on purpose, to protect the rest of the world.

Sometimes witches went bad. Sometimes they broke the number-one, inviolate rule, and had to be dealt with, sanctioned.

But I didn't believe that about Brody. I was the only one who'd seen his face that night in the mirror. I didn't believe that look of surprise and fear and naked, desperate hope could be faked.

We clasped hands as if we were shaking formally, but it didn't feel formal at all.

Quite the opposite, in fact.

A tingle started in my fingertips, shot up my arm, engulfed me, accompanied by a golden sparkly light. If this had been a movie, there would also have been the trill of a harp, or light, high bells chiming.

A warmth suffused me, despite the weather and the fact

that my hand should have been aching down to the bone. It felt like the magic of a first kiss, fresh and scary and joyously free all at the same time. Nervous anticipation and giddy delight.

And oh, so intimate.

My breath crystalized in the air before me as I whispered, "Oh, Brody."

I swear I heard a faint answer, my name caressed on his lips. "Madison."

"I'll find you, I swear," I said.

"I believe you," he said. "You've given me hope, Madison, and I wrap myself in it like a warm, safe blanket…"

His voice got fainter as he spoke, finally trailed off, and as it did, his hand slipped from mine, his fingertips brushing against my palm and fingers until they were gone.

Now the water felt icy, my hand painfully cold, and I pulled it out of the birdbath. Stared at it, and the black water that was settling back to mirror-calm. It started to snow, and fat, fluffy flakes landed on the surface, not even causing a ripple, just melting away as his hand and voice had done.

"Who *are* you?" I asked aloud, but there was no response. I hadn't expected one.

The question I didn't dare give voice to was, *And what are you doing to me?*

~

I WENT HOME for the extended holidays, and cornered my mother. Surely she would know where Grandma Belinda had gone and an easy way for me to contact her. (There were difficult, last-resort magical ways, of course.)

Whereas Grandma Belinda was chic in a caftan-wearing sort of way, my mother's chosen style was more Stevie Nicks goth chick. More traditional witch, if you think about it, by way of Victoriana. She currently wore a flowing black lace skirt, a black silk top, and pointed-toe, kitten-heeled, lace-up black boots.

I felt positively grubby in holly-print leggings and a long, berry-red cashmere tunic. I had no idea where in the house I'd kicked off my shoes.

"I assumed she really is on a cruise to Tahiti," Mom said when I asked. "If it means something else, I'm not hip to that jive."

The Tahitian government denied all knowledge of my grandmother being there, although if she'd arrived by magical means, her passport wouldn't have been recorded. Maybe her cruise ship sailed through the clouds or something. It could happen.

"I thought she would've been home for the holidays. She's never missed a Solstice before."

"No," Mom said, "she actually has on occasion, when something else has caught her attention."

"So we shouldn't be worried that we can't contact her?" I asked.

"Sweet Lord and Lady, Madison, you've met her. You know what she's like."

I thought that was a rather defeatist attitude, but I didn't say it out loud. On the other hand, at least I hadn't been raised by Grandma Belinda. I can't imagine how tiring that would be.

THAT NIGHT, I dreamed about Brody.

I'd dozed on the plane last night, but probably hadn't

slept deeply enough for a REM cycle. Contrary to popular belief, most of us prefer not to expend the extra energy, and use modern transportation methods to get from Point A to Point B. Grandma Belinda excepting. Unlike Grandma Belinda, I also hadn't perfected the art of teleportation. I'd rather take my chances hurtling through the air in a big metal bird than accidentally teleport myself into a wall, or show up in the middle of a party without my clothes.

Okay, depending on the party, that might not be awful. But still.

Tonight was the first full night's sleep I'd had since touching Brody's hand in the bird bath, since we'd, well, spoken. Not sure what else to call it. Technically we shouldn't have been able to hear each other through water —but technically, he hadn't been *in* the bird bath. The ice, the water, had been a conduit for my scrying.

The three times I'd seen him, I hadn't meant to be scrying.

I wasn't thinking about that, of course. I was asleep.

I dreamed about a door. More than half again as tall as me. Wooden, heavy, with the ornate iron hinges that extend halfway across the dark, reddish wood. There was no handle or knob or latch that I could see. Of course, the hinges were on my side, which meant the door opened out.

So I did what anybody would do in this type of dream: I knocked.

My knuckles barely made a sound, the rapping swallowed by the thick wood. No response. I knocked again. "Hello?" Then, because it fit my current obsession: "Brody?"

I had to strain to hear it, but I was sure I did when I heard my name, faintly, from behind the door.

"Madison?"

Now that I'd heard his voice, I'd know it anywhere.

Light but husky, with a bit of a raspy undertone, like a sweet, musical vibration.

Hearing it again—hearing him say my name again—sent a flash of something through me. My entire body perked up. An adrenaline rush? That would make sense. Sure, riiiight.

"Brody," I repeated. "Yes, it's Madison."

I put my hand on the door, my palm flat against the burled wood.

All I could guess was that he must've done the same, because the next thing I knew, the wood vanished, spreading away from my hand until what was beneath my skin was smooth, clear glass. And on the other side, Brody's hand, palm to palm with mine.

The glass was flawless but, I somehow knew, without even trying, unbreakable. Even our breaths didn't fog the surface. It was like looking into Snow White's coffin, except we were both standing up.

Why I didn't think it was like looking through a freaking glass door, I have no idea. That was just the first metaphor that popped into my head.

It was the first time I'd seen him clearly, not in the flickering light of a single candle or behind a fogged window. My sketches had been accurate, but only up to a point. There were so many details I'd missed.

The cowlick peaking the right side of his messy hair. (He needed a haircut. Wherever he was, maybe they didn't have barbers?) The very slight overbite.

The intensity of those ice-blue eyes.

I felt a heat in my chest, expanding out across my body like the glass had expanded to replace the wood.

"Hi," I said. "I'm dreaming. Are you?"

He nodded. "You'd think we'd be able to meet without a barrier in our dreams."

"That would make things a lot easier," I said. I could hear him just fine, though; the glass wasn't a barrier to sound, just touch. "Maybe it's an effect of the scrying. Mirrors, windows, water...those are the mediums through which I can connect with you."

"Maybe that's it. You're the first person to do that, so I have nothing to compare it to."

"Where are you?" I asked, suddenly realizing I should stop staring at those eyes and get some useful information out of this. I had so many questions. "What happened to you? When? And what's your last name? Nobody seems to recognize you and—"

"That was part of the curse," he said. "I was erased from memories."

Sweet Goddess, that was some nasty spellwork. Highly illegal stuff, too.

"I'm Brody Hawes," he added. "And I don't know where, or exactly how long ago.... Time is different here."

"Who?" I asked. "Who did this to you?"

If he knew, he didn't get the chance to tell me. My question had broken the dreamspell. Something yanked me backwards, away from the glass door, away from Brody, at the same time the same thing happened to him. I reached out, grasping, desperate, even as we whooshed away from each other into darkness...

...and then I woke up.

I tried to go back to the dream, but I wasn't a dream worker.

I slept again, but I didn't see Brody again, didn't have any dreams.

Then I smelled something heavenly...but it wasn't in a dream.

I pried my eyes open and blinked and squinted in the late morning sunlight, feeling groggy and disoriented. A hangover without the fun of a previous night's party. Ugh.

"Good morning, sunshine." Carly's voice, way too cheerful. She knew me well enough to know never to poke a sleeping Madison. I'm whatever the opposite of a morning person is, and it takes me forever to get to a point where it's safe to talk to me.

But she was also holding out a steaming mug of coffee—the source of that delicious aroma.

"Nectar of the gods," I groaned, pulling myself up enough to accept her offering. And in her defense, she hadn't spoken until I was already waking up.

My childhood bedroom wasn't full of nostalgic childhood things—I'd taken what I'd wanted when I moved out—but my mother had turned it into a guest room without really redecorating, so it still felt like mine. I'd painted it to look like a twilight forest, the walls that certain shade of blue before full darkness, the trees almost glowing. If you looked closely, you could see faeries peeking out from behind tree trunks and between leaves. The ceiling was the same blue, with shimmering golden stars.

Two twin beds, their rustic-looking headboards shaped like branches, were piled high with down blankets and pillows. Carly would take the other bed for the next few days, as she'd done all her life when she visited. She was sitting cross-legged there now, a pillow in her lap and coffee of her own in hand.

"Oh sweet Goddess, I had the weirdest dream," I said, as the disjointed memories popped up in my brain like demented gophers. Bits and pieces, slowly merging together until I mostly saw a narrative.

And along with the memory, a deep sense of loss. I didn't want to be apart from Brody. I *missed* him—wanted his presence, craved his company.

"Tell me," Carly said, intent, and I did. It was an excuse to not process the unfamiliar and confusing emotions.

"What do you think it means?" she asked when I finished.

"That I can't get this guy out of my head?" I suggested.

"Well, you *are* obsessing," she said.

"But for a good reason," I said. "He's trapped somewhere. He needs my help. Hells, who would erase him? That's borderline evil."

I put my coffee mug on the night table and sat all the way up, scrubbing my hands across my face and then through my hair. It was too early for heavy thinking, dammit.

"What's this?" Carly asked, as if she hadn't heard me. When I'd moved, something had dislodged from the tangled pile of blankets I'd been burrowing under.

One of my sketchbooks, and a handful of colored pencils.

Which I didn't remember bringing to bed with me.

The sketchbook was flipped open, past my many portrait of Brody, to a fresh page. Well, it had been fresh before I'd gone to bed. Because the book was open, the page had half torn from the spiral binding at the top, probably from being rumpled into the sheets.

And now the page was covered with an intricate symbol.

I remembered the symbol now. I remembered the door that Brody was behind had been covered with symbols.

This one, about the size of a crystal ball, had been in the center.

Exactly where I'd set my hand before the door turned clear.

There's only so much credence you could give to dreams, but this...this hadn't been a normal dream. I wasn't sure if it had been an out-of-body experience, or I'd actually traveled.... Blast and blight. I glanced down. Well, my mauve and grey fleecy pajamas weren't risqué, but they weren't exactly what I would have chosen for a first meeting with—

—with who, exactly? What did I call Brody? Who was he to me, except someone who needed my help?

That brought me around to the wringing emotions I'd been trying to bury and ignore.

I had definite feelings for Brody. His voice made my stomach flip; his gaze made my heart beat a little faster.

I didn't believe in destiny or soulmates or any of that hoohah. I believed in love, sure, but it was a mutual learning about each other and growing together.

Wasn't it?

Because this felt an awful lot like the first blushes of love.

I pressed my hand against my stomach, the coffee now burning in my gut.

"Are you okay?" Carly asked.

"No," I admitted. "And I don't think I will be until I rescue Brody."

"Who?" she asked.

A chill ran through me, colder than the icy water in the birdbath. The memory spell was more insidious than I'd realized.

∿

CARLY THOUGHT I'd been obsessing. If that were true, then what I was doing now was a million miles beyond obsession.

Now I was consumed.

My research was two-pronged: figure out who Brody was, and figure out who'd done this to him.

Then figure out how to reverse or break the spell.

I argued with myself that the urgency I felt was concern for Brody's well-being. When we were ripped apart in my dream (which, let's face it, had been much more than a simple dream), it could very well have alerted whomever cast the spell. That witch could have caused us to be ripped apart.

But the truth I didn't want to face was, I'd been drawn to Brody somehow. Only I had been able to see him. For some reason, the spell on him didn't cause me to forget him. That meant there was something special about me (not likely) or something special about *us* (more likely— and more scary).

I turned to the Annals of Magic—the massive and magical tome of our history back through time immemorial. The secret library beneath the New York Public Library was the closest place for me to access it.

The Annals lived in its own room, a circular chamber in the middle of the library with a skylight far above showing the midnight sky, even though logically there couldn't be a skylight in a library beneath another library. The young librarian who escorted me to the room wore a T-shirt that said, I'M SORRY I MISSED CHURCH—I WAS TOO BUSY PRACTICING WITCHCRAFT AND BECOMING A LESBIAN, which amused me greatly.

She left me to my research. I had to use two hands to open the heavy, scarred, brown leather cover; the book was at least two feet long, and sat on a stand on its own table of green marble, the only furniture in the room.

Of course, there were more pages than I could physically turn with my hands, because there was far more information than could fit into a physical book. I needed magic to search through the Annals.

That magic twisted and turned back on itself, fought me. No, it fought the spell on Brody. If everyone was supposed to never remember him, how could they find him in the Annals?

Because I knew whom I was looking for, though, I fought back, and won.

And then, there he was, with a picture that squeezed at my heart. His hair neatly trimmed (but still with the cowlick), his smile broad as he stood with his parents.

Brody Hawes. Son of Esme and Ignatio Hawes, of one of the most powerful witch families. The family tree went back, but not forward. Brody had been their only son. They had simply...faded away. They weren't dead, but they'd retreated from the magical community, the family gone from a dynasty to next to nothing.

They couldn't have mourned a son they didn't remember. Still, they could have had a memory of loving a child who was now lost to them. A feeling, rather than a memory. A shadow of emotion that could wrap around you like a shroud, suffocate you.

I heaved the Annals closed and leaned against the marble table, tapping my forefinger against my teeth.

I could go to Brody's parents, but the likelihood was slim that me being able to see and talk to him would dent the spell that kept them from remembering him. If they didn't remember him, then some crazy witchling from an unimportant family showing up on their doorstep babbling about a son they didn't know anything about would be... beyond awkward, at the very least.

Well, at least I knew who Brody was. Step two of my cunning plan was to figure out who had done this to him.

Since nobody remembered him, I couldn't ask who might have wanted to take Brody down. Now that I thought about it, the goal might have been to dethrone his powerful family.

If I started asking around about that, I ran the risk of stirring up a basilisk nest of trouble. The only thing I had going for me right now was that very few people knew that I knew about Brody. Well, I'd circulated his sketch...that could come back to bite me on the patootie.

Fairyfarts. I hadn't thought about that until now, either.

I was probably on somebody's magical radar, then.

That made all the more determined to rescue him. It added urgency to a situation already powered by stubbornness and that other feeling I was refusing to name aloud.

So now what?

I had one final clue left: the sigil. It was on the door that kept Brody trapped in what amounted to another dimension. Magic like that wasn't a one-time spell; it was something that needed to be maintained, constantly monitored. That was one of the reasons it was so insidious: This was no crime of passion. This was ongoing wrath, revenge.

Which meant that someone carried that sigil with them —a tattoo, an amulet, or something else they didn't go far from.

Who, I wondered, loathed Brody or his family so completely?

The Annals of Magic wouldn't be any help in this situation.

I had to find the sigil.

~

I WENT BACK HOME—I was still on vacation—and prepared a seeking spell.

I stationed Carly outside my room, just in case. Inside, I swept the magic circle on the bedroom floor (there was one in every room of the house) with a special broom, banishing any stray negative energy and dust bunnies (those puppies can really make a spell go awry).

Fat white candles in the four quarters, and four chunks of amethyst spaced between them. A circle of salt and rosemary sprinkled around the perimeter. I sat cross-legged in the center with my sketch of the sigil in my lap.

I didn't have any sketches of Brody with me, because I didn't want to go to him. Well, I *did*, but that wasn't the purpose of this spell. Seeing the sigil on the door that trapped him wasn't going to help me, or him. I had to learn where the sigil originated.

In the candlelight, the fairies painted on the wall seemed to flit between the trees. Or maybe those were real fairies. In any case, they were never any help. They had their own rules about how the world worked, like leaving money in exchange for lost body parts. (Teeth are just the tip of the iceberg. Ever find loose change on the ground? Count your eyelashes.)

I took seven slow breaths and out, taking in air scented with candlewax and rosemary, then dropped my head and stared at the sigil until my vision blurred and my consciousness loosened from my physical body.

Up and out. For a moment I hovered over myself, looking down. My posture sucked and I'd missed a spot in the back when I'd brushed my hair this morning.

Focus, dammit.

I looked at the sigil, committed it to memory, placed it firmly in my mind so it drove out other thoughts and ideas and mental pictures. No Madison distractions. Only sigil.

Then I was away and flying.

I swooped and soared, faster than I could process. Apparently the sigil wasn't that hard to find, because I was shooting like an arrow, like an osprey dropping from the sky.

When I could see again, I realized I was hovering over the Charles estate. The vast grounds were still, of course, covered in a fresh dusting of snow. So pretty and peaceful, and even though my body was back in my bedroom, I swore I could feel the energy of the Solstice ritual shimmering over the place.

I cursed. Apparently I was distracted after all, because I'd come to a place that made me happy, not to mention the place where I'd first touched Brody.

I focused on the sigil again, but I didn't leave. I held steady, looking down at the woods surrounding the massive house that always reminded me of Tara on steroids, at the fountains and orchard and gardens and...

I sucked in a breath, or whatever the bodiless equivalent of sucking in a breath was.

The knot garden. The intricate growth of hedges that were designed to be viewed from above, but the only way to see the pattern was to stand on the balcony on the third floor of the house, which wasn't open to guests.

Well, that wasn't the only way. I'd found another way to see the pattern.

The knot garden's pattern was the sigil that bound Brody and kept him from everyone's memories.

The concept that someone in that house was responsible, someone whom I'd met, freaked me out so much I lost my control of my soul-flying. My at-home body sucked my consciousness back so fast, it felt as if it took no longer than a blink.

As soon as I snapped back into my body, I scrambled to my feet, the sketch of the sigil falling to the floor. Wooh, too soon after soul-flying. My vision darkened around the edges and my head felt woozy. I sucked in air, and energy from the earth and sky, and thankfully didn't pass out, although it was touch-and-go for a moment there.

"Carly!" I shouted.

The door banged open to reveal Carly, her eyes wide. "911 or your parents?" she asked, brandishing her cell phone.

"Neither," I said. "I need to talk to Grandma Belinda, whatever it takes. This is an emergency."

To contact someone at a distance, you put three of their favorite things in a sacred circle. In this case, that meant a vodka tonic (double the vodka), a photo of Burt Reynolds, and rose-petal hand cream made by Persian imps.

It wasn't an easy spell, not to mention I was already tired from the soul-flying. More importantly, it wasn't to be used lightly. You weren't just calling someone, you were yanking them to you, and that's rude at best. At worst, it's a violation.

I had no other choice. And, I feared, neither did Brody.

The Annals held our history. Grandma Belinda knew all our gossip.

What I got was Grandma Belinda's floating head about two feet from mine. I was glad it was just her head, because I had the distinct impression she wasn't wearing any clothes.

It didn't matter. I was so relieved to see her, I almost cried.

A hand appeared, plucked the vape cigarette from her mouth, and disappeared. She must've seen the expression on my face, because her own expression softened from her initial scowl and she said, "What is it, darling?"

I cut right to the chase, which I knew she'd appreciate. "Does the Charles family have some sort of problem with the Hawses?"

"Oh my Goddess and God!" The hand and vape appeared briefly again as she waved them around. "Now *that's* a situation full of unicorn pucky. The Charleses and the Hawses have been polite frenemies for centuries."

"I'm thinking something recent."

"Then you mean the scandal when Freddy Charles decided he was ass over teakettle in love with Esme Hawes —despite the fact that she was Esme *Hawes* and *married* to Ignatio Hawes."

"Tawdry affair?" I guessed.

Grandma Belinda snorted. "Hardly, darling. Esme and Ignatio were a love match for the ages. She wanted nothing to do with Freddy, and who could blame her? He wasn't just ass over teakettle—he was a grade-A *ass*."

"Wait..." Suddenly it clicked together. "*Frederick* Charles, the current head of the Charles family? The one who hosts Solstice?" I'd met him only once, the first year I was allowed to go to Solstice. He was tall and genteel, still hale and strong despite a full head of thick white hair. But his eyes were so dark brown they looked almost black, and I hadn't liked the way he looked at me—looked at everyone, really—and after he'd shaken my hand, I'd felt unsettled.

At the time, I'd chalked it up to scary excitement over my first major ritual.

Now, it seemed, I'd just been reacting to the scary.

Because what he'd done to Brody and Brody's family was *terrifying*.

"One and the same," she said. "I've had to beat him away with a broomstick a few times. The man doesn't take *no* for an answer very well. Just doesn't hear it."

That was also terrifying: if he'd pursued Grandma Belinda with the fervor he'd shown Esme Hawes, *I* might be the one trapped who-knows-where.

"Grandma," I said carefully, "this is about Brody Hawes."

"Who's Brody Hawes?" she asked.

"Esme and Ignatio's son."

If I hadn't known her so well, I might have missed the fraction-of-a-second of blankness that crossed her gaze. "Esme and Ignatio don't have a son named Brody, darling. You must be mistaken."

"Just seeing if you were paying attention," I said, because I didn't want to trigger that look again. "Different Brody."

"What does this have to do with the Charleses and the Hawses, then?"

"Nothing," I said. "Never mind. My brain's all over the place today."

Grandma Belinda's demeanor changed suddenly, and she peered at me, eyes intent. "You're in love, aren't you?"

"No." Yes. *Dammit.*

"Don't try to bamboozle me, darling—I'm the master at it and can see right through you. So what's the matter?"

I could lie to myself (badly), but she was right: I couldn't lie to her. I thought about how to phrase things so she'd hear them. "He's trapped by a spell."

"Ohhhh." She let the word out on a long breath, one that would no doubt have bathed me in vodka fumes had she actually been in the room with me. "Well, then, you're the perfect person to rescue him."

"I am?"

"Did you not listen to the fairy tales I read to you? Hecate's ass, girl."

She looked as though she was about to say more, but something caught her attention and she turned her head. I heard "My granddaughter. Love. Spell. No, not a love spell —" She made a noise that distinctly sounded like a girlish giggle, which was unnerving, then turned back to me. "Got to go, darling. Good luck. You've got more power than you realize. Love to all. Mwah!"

With an audible *pop*, she vanished, my spell broken. The highball glass was empty, and the photo and hand cream were gone.

So was my energy. I wanted nothing more than to crawl into bed, and I felt as though I could sleep for a week. Or a century, like Sleeping Beauty.

Problem was, my visit to Brody and my soul-flying to find the sigil could have alerted Frederick Charles, and I had a bad feeling I had to act *now*.

On the upside, the longest I'd been able to speak to him had been via a dream, so I *was* going to get some sleep.

It just wasn't going to be very restful.

My next concern was for my family. It would be smart, I knew, to have magical backup—even just to let everyone know what was going on, as best I could without tripping the forgetting-Brody spell. But the more they knew, the more danger they might be in. If Frederick Charles (I couldn't bring myself to think of him as Freddy) turned his wrath on me, that was because I'd chosen to poke the basilisk nest. I didn't want my parents or Carly or anyone in the crossfire.

Since everyone else was still out, I convinced Carly to watch a nail-biter of a movie with me, then halfway through claimed a headache and said I was going to bed. I knew her. She couldn't turn the movie off without seeing the end.

After pondering what pajamas were appropriate for a rescue, and deciding jeans made more practical sense, I snuggled down under the down comforters. Being horizontal and comfy felt blissful. I'd taken my favorite sketch of Brody with me, and set my sketchbook and pencils next to me just in case. Closing my eyes, I focused on him, and the door with the sigil, and made my intent clear.

My last conscious thought was that I had no bloody clue what Grandma Belinda meant by the fairy tale comment, but it would make sense when I needed it to.

I hoped.

I HAVE TO ADMIT, I was sort of surprised to find myself at the same wooden door as before. I would've thought Frederick would've blocked me from it. Maybe he wasn't as powerful as I thought—or maybe he wasn't paying close enough attention.

Or maybe this was a trap.

Oh well, too late now. I was in it to win it.

"Brody!" I shouted. "Brace yourself."

I placed my hand flat on the door again, on the sigil, and the wood vanished outward, replaced by glass.

Brody was there. Again we were palm to palm.

He looked expectant, and I belatedly remembered I didn't have a clue what to do next.

Fairy tales. I'd thought of the glass door as Snow White's coffin, hadn't I? How had her Prince had gotten the coffin open? Disney never explained that, did they? (Oh Disney, you were wrong about so many things. Fairy godmothers especially. Yeesh.) I closed my eyes, letting all the myths and stories swirl in my brain, random and half-formed, snatches of images and sentences and concepts.

Doors and mirrors. Roses and music. Snow and ice. In "The Snow Queen," Kay has a shard of magical ice in his eye and his sister, Gerda, cries and melts it. I didn't think I had enough moisture in me to weep Brody's way to freedom.

Okay, what else? Fairy tales were about truth, and doing the right thing. Dammit, I was *trying* to do the right thing. Truth. Love. True love. True love's kiss...

If I'd stopped to think, I would've run away screaming. Thankfully, I didn't think at all. I just let myself feel.

I leaned towards the glass, and saw before my eyes fluttered shut that Brody did the same on the other side.

I'd punched through the ice in the birdbath. Now I warmed the glass with my breath...and it melted away, until Brody and I touched once again.

Lip to lip, in a kiss.

He was warm, and his messy hair smelled like sunshine, and for a moment I quite happily forgot about any danger, about why I was even there, because it seemed obvious that I was there to enjoy this very tingle-inducing kiss. The door was gone, and I was in Brody's arms. They were strong around me. I had a feeling he hadn't felt another human's touch in a long time, but it was more than that. The kiss was more than that.

I knew it right down into my bones.

This time, when I felt the yank backwards and heard the whooshing, I held on to him with everything I had. The wind, or something, tried to tear him away, and I fought, clinging to him in an embrace that would have been intimate if it weren't a probable matter of life and death....

I woke with a jolt. My eyes flew open in a panic before I fully registered where I was...and who I was with.

Brody and I were still wrapped around each other.

At least we were clothed. Not that I'm against nudity, mind you, but a little foreplay would be nice first.

He was smiling at me, those sea-glass blue eyes filled with wonder. "Hi," he said.

"Hi," I said.

"So, usually I like to get to know a girl a little better before..." He gestured, encompassing the bed and our position in it.

"Yeah, well, our dates *have* been a little unconventional," I said, trying not to think about how our legs were entwined and what bits were pressed up against other bits. Again, not a prude, but the conflicting emotions battling inside me were, well, conflicting me. My body was interested, but my brain pointed out I didn't know this guy, but my heart suggested maybe I knew him better than my brain thought I did.

I didn't believe in destiny or fate. That wasn't what magic was about.

"Hell of a story to tell our kids," he said.

"Woah. Woah!" I pulled away from him, pressing back against the wall, fighting off panic.

"You're right: too soon." His smile had faded. "I'm sorry. My brain is completely addled right now. I can't believe I'm here. In the real world, I mean, not your bed specifically. I should be asking what year it is, and whether my parents are still alive, and who's the head of the Council."

My heart slowed a little. "Your parents are still alive," I said, realizing the enormity of that question. "And I'm thinking that if you're here, the spell is broken, and they remember you again."

In that case, he needed to call them, and all hell was going to break loose. A moment later, I heard the front door open, and the babble of my family's voices: parents, Carly, her parents, and...Grandma Belinda?

All hell was about to break loose in a different way. How to explain my relationship with Brody to my parents? Would Grandma Belinda tell them I was in love?

Brody slid out from under the covers and held out a hand to me. I reached for it, already missing the warmth of his body, already wishing we'd had a few more moments to talk.

Oh, I had it bad. Yes I did. And at that moment, the concept of that was even more terrifying than the cold wrath and evil magic of Frederick Charles.

ONCE THE SPELL WAS BROKEN, the Magical Council had a collective hippogriff. People remembered Brody now, and realized what Frederick Charles had done and how many laws he'd broken. Esme and Ignatio almost burned down the Charles estate trying to get at Frederick, but thankfully the Council scooped him up before any lives or houses were lost.

It was soon clear that nobody else in the Charles family had been aware or part of what Frederick had done, but I was willing to put money on the fact they weren't going to be hosting Solstice for a while. Pity, because I really did love those gardens.

Nasty sigil knotwork garden excepting.

As for me, I practically *did* run screaming. I didn't scream, but I ran. I had all these feelings for a man I didn't know, a man who seemed quite nice and quite interested in me, but maybe that was because I'd saved his life and all that. Or was it?

The problem wrapped around to the first time I'd seen Brody: in the hand mirror when Carly and I were drunk and trying out the scrying spell to find your one true love.

Obviously I believed in magic—and love. I just didn't believe in love manipulated by magic. That was just as nasty as what Frederick had done to Brody (and to Esme and Ignatio, who'd nearly lost their minds to a grief they couldn't identify).

Brody was sweet and patient and nonstalkerish, as well as clearly interested in getting to know me, suggesting we start from square one, as if we'd just met. As if it were that simple.

I was honest with him: I didn't want him to feel manipulated.

"Believe me," he said, "I know what that feels like, and this isn't it."

But...but...argh!

When I'd had enough of agonizing over it all, and enough of hiding from poor Brody, who swore he just wanted to spend casual, non-pressured time with me, I pulled on my big-girl panties and went to see Grandma Belinda. She was back from Tahiti (or wherever she'd been;

she still wouldn't confirm or deny) and settling into her new condo in the Hamptons.

It smelled like clean sea air rather than cigarettes, and was a far cry from the 1970s ranch, with a gleaming all-white kitchen (despite her disinterest in cooking) and a wall of windows in the living room looking out at the beach. Apparently Grandma Belinda was taking up painting. I glanced at the canvas on the easel by the window and regretted it. I did *not* need to know that about her and her companion. Or Burt Reynolds. It was hard to tell.

I shook my head and thrust *How to Find Your One True Love Through Magic* at her.

"I wondered where that had gotten to." Grandma Belinda switched her vape to the other hand so she could open the book. "Your grandfather gave it to me. Said he'd used this mirror-and-candle thing and seen me, and knew I was the one for him." She snorted. "Can you imagine? Buncha drunk frat boys prancing backwards up a staircase in the dark. It's a wonder he didn't break his damn fool neck."

"But...but I thought we couldn't see the future. That the future wasn't set in stone, and..."

She looked at me. "We can't, and it isn't," she said. "That's not what scrying's about; that's not what the spell is about. It's just a..." She waved her hand. "Okay. Look. Just because he saw me in the mirror doesn't mean we were destined to be together. It just meant we were compatible. That we had a strong connection. It's what you *do* with that kind of information that's important. It didn't mean I was going to fall head-over-heels at first glimpse of him. He still had to be a good person. He still had to woo me."

The wicked grin she gave then made me very much not want to know how he wooed her.

"I mean, he coulda been an asshole. True love exists, Madison, but that doesn't mean you don't have to work at it. Nobody's perfect, and no relationship is perfect, and you've still gotta fight for it. It's about whether you're willing to walk through fire for the other person, you know?"

Oh. I knew, all right.

"Thanks for finding this," she added, tucking the book away. "I meant to keep it."

I slowly walked outside and down the sand, warmer beneath my bare feet than it ought to have been for late winter on Long Island, but that was Grandma Belinda for you: buy a condo on Long Island but spell the beach to be like Miami. At the water's edge, I dropped down, pulling my legs to my chest and wrapping my arms around my knees.

My stomach churned, not in a nauseated way, but in a scared-but-maybe-excited way. Or maybe in a love way.

I knew how I reacted to the sound of Brody's voice, the sight of his eyes the color of the ocean before me, and quirk of his mouth and the bridge of his nose. I knew having a heart-squeezing reaction to the bridge of his nose was bordering on crazysauce.

I sucked in a deep breath of salty air. I knew I was in love with him, at least the parts of him I knew and liked.

It was, as Grandma Belinda said, what I *did* with that information that was important.

What I needed to do with it was give Brody a chance.

I had a sneaking suspicion he was up to the challenge.

I glanced back at the house. Grandma Belinda, at the window, waved, and then she and the easel and her painting supplies vanished. Message received, Grandma Belinda. Thanks.

I pulled out my cell phone. "Brody? It's Madison. I'd like to...to talk. Are you free to come to Long Island? I have the run of a sweet beach house for a little while...."

The second rule of magic didn't count when it came to love, because being clear of mind isn't exactly what love is about.

THE MADNESS OF SURVIVAL

Suddenly awake, I stared into the darkness, all senses straining to figure out what had woken me.

The clock LED gleamed just past midnight. The trick-or-treaters were snuggled in their beds, the partiers hadn't yet stumbled home. Only the faint occasional hum of a car broke the silence. Santa Barbara in autumn was just barely cool enough to close the windows at night, and I had a light comforter pulled over Shawn and me.

Eva was sleeping through the night now, but I was still breastfeeding, the milky scent clinging to my body.

Had Eva made a noise? I listened, heard nothing.

A mother's instinct was what pulled me from beneath the covers. Barefoot in a pair of cotton pajama pants dotted with flowers and a pale pink tank top that didn't remotely match any colors in the pants, I walked to the bedroom doorway. I didn't need to turn on a light.

In the bed, Shawn stirred. "Alis? 'kay?"

"Just checking on…"

Framed in the doorway, I smelled it. Tasted it.

Faerie glamour.

Spun sugar, too sweet. Like walking through cobwebs the consistency of cotton candy.

"...Eva," I whispered, fighting through the strands. Then I could move at normal speed again (How long had it taken me to get from the bed to the doorway? How long had it taken me to even wake up?), and I ran into the next room. Hit the light switch shaped like a sheep. Three long steps to the crib.

Some disconnected part of me noted that the wail emerging from my lungs sounded unearthly. Inhuman.

Despairing.

WINTER SOLSTICE IN SANTA BARBARA, California. A balmy 50 degrees on the longest night of the year. Never a wish of snow in the air, and I wouldn't have been surprised if some fool had been out surfing today.

I've lived here for twenty years and it still seemed wrong. My very ex-husband, Shawn, who'd spent his whole life in Southern California, thought it was normal to wear shorts on Christmas Day. Didn't see anything wrong with wrapping strands of lights around a palm tree.

Now, as my motorcycle slipped through the dark, arid streets, I ached for the fresh linen scent of snow. My ex had said snow stayed in the mountains where it belonged, and we could visit it. I'd said I wanted our daughter to know the magic of waking up on Christmas morning and seeing the great white flakes drifting down.

But then Eva was gone, and my ex soon thereafter. Death of a child is hard on any marriage, but when you can't explain why you're reacting the way you are...

When the Fae take a human child, they leave a

changeling. Sometimes that changeling isn't a living thing —that explains, for example, SIDS. To the human eye, there's a baby who died an unexplained death. To anyone able to see through Faerie glamour, all that lies in the crib is a bundle of twigs.

I could see through the glamour. Thankfully I was smart enough not to tell anyone past my first, initial hysteria—a hysteria that was chalked up to a mother's fresh grief.

Sometimes the Fae leave one of their own Faerie children, which will be sickly and pale because we don't have the right food in the human world, although fresh, whole cream and oats and pomegranate seeds, and leeks sautéed in butter, will help. That's apparently what happened with me, when I was taken as a child—which is why I was able to fight my way out, sending my faerie doppelgänger back home. I imagine she fared better than I did.

Then again, the Fae are cruel and capricious, and may have taken out their anger at losing me on her.

As far as I know—as far as any of us know—children exchanged for bundles of twigs never return.

It's probably madness that lets me believe I'll see Eva again. I desperately hope she won't be broken; hope that because of my own experience and understanding, I'll be able to ease her through the transition.

Most of us are some level of broken.

The madness that allowed us to survive in Faerie.

We—the group of us that ride together and protect children from the Fae—have hints of leftover magic. Our motorcycles make no sound to the human ear, seem to have a dusting of *don't-look-here* about them, allowing us to slip in and out of traffic, make our way through the city without notice. Or, if someone does notice us—someone who also has the mark of the Fae upon them, perhaps—they forget quickly.

The rheumy-eyed homeless man, grey in his tattered tweed coat and unraveling fingerless gloves, eyes me from his spot tucked into the bank steps as I idle at a stop sign. He turns to his companion and says, "Did you see—?" and then I'm gone and his companion asks, "What?" and he shakes his head and mutters.

Joe-Joe, who survived being conscripted into the Wild Hunt, opines that the bikes are ensorcelled faerie steeds. Sometimes I feel as though mine's alive—I can't say why I have the habit of running my hand along her chrome flanks as if soothing her—but I'm not sure.

My time in Faerie taught me to question everything, believe nothing.

My motorcycle was a small cruiser, comfortable and low enough for me to plant my feet firmly on the ground when needed. I called her Asfaloth, like the horse Glorfindel rode in *The Lord of the Rings*, who carried Frodo from the Ringwraiths.

Fast, brave, and able to outrun evil.

You might think I'd shy away from a name like that, but Tolkien's Elves are nothing like the Fae. And besides, the steeds were never malevolent.

If magic is real, I had to believe there was good magic.

We're like the Lost Boys and Lost Girls, like war-torn orphans in a country we've never seen before. We've had experiences few people understood—few people would even believe was real. You can't explain to a psychiatrist that your PTSD isn't from a tour in the Middle East, but in the wars between Light and Dark Fae, between Good and Evil, and you never volunteered to serve.

That the howl of a dog sends you into a sweating, trembling panic, not because you'd been bit, or menaced by a stray pack, but because the sound is a pale echo of the hounds baying in the Wild Hunt—and you'd angered the Queen and had been ensorcelled to run *as* one of her jet-black hounds.

We couldn't find empathy from anyone except those who'd experienced the same thing. Slowly we banded together, a gang from the outside, perhaps. But a family from the inside. A family made up of the ragged, the broken, the formerly bespelled, helping one another heal.

And protecting children from being taken like we were.

I PULLED up in front of a California bungalow home, a gabled, two-story construction painted a classic sage green with brick red and cream accents. Fat square wooden columns, narrowing as they rose, held up the wide porch roof. Fragrant pink flowers spilled from baskets hanging along the eaves. This late at night, the only light on was the porch light, shaped like a lantern.

I was off my bike and backing away, chanting "No, no, no" before I even realized I was doing it.

I knew this house. Knew who lived there.

Joe-Joe was already there, and Parvo, and Sunny. Joe-Joe, the nominal leader of our group, was the one who came over to me, holding out his hand as if to sooth a skittish horse; then, once he was sure I wouldn't bolt, resting his hand gently on my shoulder.

"Alis? What's up?" he asked.

Joe-Joe rides a Harley, and looked like a typical rider except that he's smart enough to wear a full helmet, not one of those little Nazi-esqe beanies with a spike on top that wouldn't protect a watermelon being thrown down on the pavement. He was tall and burly, with scraggly hair and an even scragglier beard. If you could get past that, though, his hazel eyes were kind, always kind, despite a hint of despair behind them.

He had been in Faerie the longest of all of us, and has the knack to know which kids the Fae will be targeting. He's the one who tells us where to go. I don't know how many jobs we all had tonight, in Santa Barbara and down the coast into Ventura and Oxnard. As with Halloween and the Summer Solstice and the equinoxes, it was one of the busiest nights of the year.

Certainly enough for all of us to have one, maybe two rescues to handle.

We work in teams of two, one person outside in the hopes of stopping the Fae if they came that way, or distracting anyone else who might try to enter the house, and one person inside, the last line of defense for the child against the kidnappers.

I unbuckled my own helmet and tugged it off. The cool breeze ruffled my hair. I kept it in a dark tight braid, because nothing tangles hair better than wind when you're riding. All those movies and commercials where a woman removes a motorcycle helmet and shakes her head and her perfect hair comes cascading down? Bullshit.

Even my braid probably looked like ass right now, matted down, wisping out. I shoved the bangs off my forehead, took a deep, deep breath.

Eased the air out through my teeth, counting down, calming.

"I don't know if I can do this," I said.

Joe-Joe waited. Patient. I'd talk when I was ready.

But he also knew, just as I did, that it was nearing midnight on the Winter Solstice, the longest night of the year and one of the times when the Veil between the Worlds is thin, and the Fae come out to play and steal their latest crop of toys.

We didn't have much time.

Inside, little Noah, age 4, slumbered peacefully away, unaware of the fate that would befall him—unless we got inside and stopped it.

Inside, my former best friend, Grace, slumbered peacefully away as well, trapped in the cotton-candy gauze of faerie glamour.

We had been friends pretty much since I'd returned from Faerie. She'd never been. Our mutual love of folklore, myth, and fantasy stemmed from different desires: she wanted to escape the real world, whereas I wanted to understand the world I'd escaped from. She never knew about my past.

Which was probably why she turned her back on me after Eva was taken. Pretty much everyone did, because who wanted to stick by a woman who insisted her dead child wasn't dead? Eva's death was ruled as SIDS; any questionable charges against me were dropped. I pulled my crazy together, just barely, but by that time Shawn had filed for divorce and taken off, and even Grace, my oldest friend, mumbled something about "nothing in common anymore."

Which translated to "I have to protect my own child from the crazy."

And now I was expected to protect Noah? Was this irony, or design?

We don't know how the Fae choose children.

Not many people escape from Faerie, so my own situation was especially unusual, a returnee—an anomaly—who then has child taken by the Fae.

This…gang/family/group had spent a lot of time helping me with the guilt that the Fae had taken Eva as payback for losing me. Whether or not that was true, I still suffered the guilt.

The Fae were capricious, cold, but in some ways, not calculating. They held grudges, oh, yes they did—their feuds lasted centuries—but by the same token, they moved slower than humans did. My time with them was a blink of an eye, like owning a goldfish.

There was no way to know.

Question everything, believe nothing.

Now, while I dithered, Noah could be lost.

No matter how Grace felt about me, no matter that a two-decades-old friendship had shattered in flames, I couldn't do that to Noah.

I couldn't do it to any child, but especially not to one I knew and, despite everything, loved.

Joe-Joe waited, patient, for my explanation.

My hands shook. I wanted to rest them on Asfaloth's tank, soak in the warmth, the safety. Astride her, I felt invincible. Like I could outrun my fears.

I understood now I had to face those fears.

"I'm okay," I said. Deep breath in through the nose, out through the teeth. Had the temperature dropped? I dug my hands into the pockets of my brown leather jacket for warmth and solidity. "I know the people who live here. We…have a history."

"You sure?" he asked, his deep voice rumbling with sympathy and support. "Sunny and I have another house nearby, but Parvo can take point, or we can swap…"

I shook my head, stripping off my leather gloves. Parvo was like *that* uncle, the one who's normal most of the time, but you know he's skittish and you avoid certain topics or sudden loud sounds around him. He was slender and small, with close-cropped greying hair, and hell, he made *me* nervous.

He was far, far better outside, as the first line of defense.

And there wasn't time to swap houses or teams.

"I'll be okay," I reiterated. "You go. Call me if another job comes up."

We were scattered throughout Santa Barbara, a ragtag, scruffy-looking group of bikers, a family held together by our bikes and the taint of faerie magic we just couldn't scrub off, no matter how many times we showered or surrounded ourselves with iron.

And by the resolve we held to protect, no matter what the cost.

I BUMPED fists with Parvo and went in.

Inside, the house smelled of coconut milk and Chinese five spice and lemongrass. Grace had always loved to cook; had fallen easily into the role of wife and mother. Maybe that's what started the decline of our friendship: she judged me for falling back on Easy Mac, for wanting to go back to work after Eva was a few months old. (Not that I'd had the chance...)

I shook myself—I really did, a head-to-toe shuddering release. Glamour had a way of making you feel inadequate. Bad about yourself. Susceptible to other forces. To being led away, led astray...

There are a few tales of adults being coerced into the

Faerie realm. *Tam Lin*'s one of the most famous, but there are others involving faerie rings and standing stones and being in the wrong place at the wrong time and seeing the Wild Hunt ride by as a beautiful, glittering, magical spectacle rather than the dark despair it really is.

I would not get suckered in, not here, not now.

If I went back in blinded, I'd never find my way out again. Never find my daughter, never return to the real world.

People think Faerie must be breathtakingly lovely and perfect. In some ways, there's perfection, but it's cold. Not cold as in frigid, but cold in the sense of both temperature and emotion. You're never truly warm in Faerie; even the fires burn blue and give off no heat. The land is in perpetual twilight; if you even make it outside, you'll find no sun.

And the Fae themselves? Disaffected, distant. Immortality breeds ennui.

Ice can be breathtaking, but when you shatter it, there's nothing behind it.

The scent of fresh Thai food faded as I ascended the wooden staircase, remembering even now which riser creaked if you stepped in the center. There wasn't much need to avoid it; Grace and her husband would be glamoured, and if Noah were awake, that could make things even easier.

Children have a magic of their own, and with protection, they can help ward off the Fae.

By the time I got to the top of the stairs, the homey smells of cooking had been replaced by sweet cotton candy laced with the ashes of snowflakes.

I paused outside the master bedroom, the reddish-stained five-panel door open just a crack, but then I pressed on through the sickly webbing of glamour. I didn't need to see Grace and her husband. Didn't need to see the pale yellow of her bedroom walls, a paint color that soaked up the golden California sunshine and made the room bright and airy—a color I'd suggested, and helped roll onto those very walls.

Didn't want to gloat and think *See, see? It could happen to anyone.*

The bedrooms were arrayed around a central landing. Noah's was catty-corner from his parents'. His door was also cracked open, the faint blue-green glow of a nightlight leaking out.

I pushed the door the rest of the way open, pushed through the strongest glamour woven across the doorway, that disgusting, clinging cobwebby cotton-candy stickiness.

The last time I'd been here, it had been a baby's room. Now it was a little boy's room, and Noah apparently loved the ocean. The nightlight was a dolphin, a bedside lamp was a smiling octopus holding up a bulb at the end of each of its legs, and one wall was a mural of sea creatures above and below the surface, some of which glowed in the dark.

The crib had been replaced by a bed, and there was Noah, dark hair rumpled, his face round and cherubic, his skin pale and smooth.

I had only the flash of a moment to admire him, to experience the regret of not seeing him grow from baby to preschooler, before the Fae arrived.

I'd known it would be soon, given the thickness of the glamour I'd fought through. I was more prepared for them than I'd been for seeing Noah.

They wove their doorway out of shadows, between one breath and the next. I'd noticed in the past, as I did now, that they tended to create them as close to a human doorway as possible; perhaps that made the magic easier.

It also explained the monsters-in-the-closet problem.

Two Fae stepped through. Tall, cold, slender, beautiful, terrible. They shone with their own luminosity, and it took me a moment to adjust my sight.

Still, I faced them, placing myself between them and Noah.

"This child is not for you to take," I said.

The one in front, with long, pale hair the color of moonlit tears, cocked his head. "On whose authority?"

"All humanity," I said. "Human children are not playthings to be stolen away for your amusement. You may not come into our world and kidnap at will."

"You think it is at will?" he said, and took one, achingly graceful step to the side, so I could see the second Fae who'd accompanied him.

For the briefest of moments, my brain scrambled to understand, to come up with the simplest solution, which was that there'd been a mirror on the closet door that I hadn't noticed.

But I'm not vain enough to think I could ever be so stunning.

Or so soulless.

She was my doppelgänger.

I remember my time in Faerie very, very well. I remember fighting to get out, every chance I got.

I don't remember getting out, or seeing my shadow, my other self, in this world.

"So," she said. "Finally, we meet."

Her hair was long and dark, a long, graceful braid down her back, where mine was haphazard and matted. Her eyes were an ocean of blue mine could never attain.

It didn't matter. I didn't want to be her, and I didn't want to be where she was from.

I felt as if I'd been punched in the stomach, had the wind knocked out of me, but I still took a step closer, wanting to see her more clearly.

Drawn, in hindsight, into the glamour of her own making. Of our own making.

"Are you...okay?" I had to ask. "Did my getting out, forcing you to return to Faerie...was that bad for you?"

She laughed, but it was the farthest thing from humor you or I or anyone could imagine.

"You humans and your concern, your care," she said. "Your *honor*." She said the word as if it tasted bad on her tongue. "It will always be your downfall."

And then, yes, she was right, I realized my mistake. I'd let her distract me.

While the other one grabbed Noah.

He was around me in a blink of an eye, a movement I could see only because of the time I'd spent in their world, the same way I could recognize their glamour. But I wasn't as fast as they were.

My twin smiled without any emotion except some hideous mix of triumph and pity.

"Good-bye, sister," she said. "Enjoy the life you have here." She stepped backwards through the doorway, vanished.

The Fae holding Noah stepped through as well.

I didn't have time to think, to process, to consider. I had time only to do what was right.

I dove after them. After Noah.

She was right. Our honor would be our downfall.

Thing was, ever since Eva was taken, I'd tried to find a way back into Faerie. A way to enter with my full faculties intact, not enchanted and dazed by glamour. Maybe I hadn't been looking in the right place—or maybe I'd never had the courage.

All I knew was that right now, I had to save Noah.

Faerie doorways are never simple; they're not a step between one world and the other. They're passageways. Dark, cold places full of disorienting magic, designed to get you lost forever.

I didn't even get fully inside. If I had, things might have gone differently. I might have made different choices.

I didn't realize right then that I had a choice. All I knew was the job I'd sworn to do...the child I'd promised to protect.

I got in just far enough to reach them, to feel the bone-chilling cold, and I snatched Noah out of the Fae's arms and backpedaled as fast as I could, and then I was falling to the wood floor, the breath knocked out of me as my back slammed down, and I through a haze of stars I saw the doorway close. The veil thickened. It was past midnight.

I didn't have much time.

Noah was still under the glamour, so I scrambled up and tucked him haphazardly under the covers. Then I was running down the stairs as the glamour faded behind me. They'd wake up any second now.

At least Grace and her husband would find Noah safe in his bed. If they even woke up at all, sensed anything had changed.

I flashed a thumbs-up at Parvo. Then I jammed my helmet on, buckled it with shaking fingers, twisted the key. Asfaloth answered with a rumbling purr only I could hear.

"We can get into Faerie," I told her, my voice small. Then I repeated, louder, "We can get into Faerie. We just have to find the door. I know you'll help me with that."

I knew I should tell Joe-Joe, Parvo, any one of the others, where I was going, what I was going to try to do. But I had to go, had to try, before I lost faith.

I had to cling to the madness to survive.

I'm given to understand that no matter where you cross, you end up in the mythology of your own people—your ancestral DNA, sort of. Doorways to Faerie can be accessed anywhere; you didn't have to be in Britain to find the portals to Celtic deities, or in Greece to find that pantheon's arches.

In the Southern California desert—and it's all desert, right down to the ocean's edge, no matter how hard people have tried to build Los Angeles into an oasis—you'd expect the doorways to open into a Native American dreamworld. But even the Coyote doesn't steal babies while he forces their parents to slumber.

Now I knew I could reach through, touch the Faerie lands.

Now I knew I could get back in and find Eva.

In Grace's house, the Fae had opened the doorway. I'd sacrificed my chance in exchange for saving Noah.

I didn't have the power to open a doorway, but doorways existed. And Asfaloth could help me find one.

I pulled out into the suburban street, headed for the freeway. The 101 South to the 33 North through the mountains, then beyond.

We were going out into the desert, my motorcycle steed and I. We were riding through the longest night of the year until we found the weak spot between the worlds.

We'd make that weak spot a doorway.

And we would go through, and I would find a way to bring Eva home.

LEAVE A CANDLE BURNING

She was lost.

Claudia stopped in the tree-lined lane, surrounded by the deep blue of twilight, a swirl of snowflakes, and an ever-growing drift of snow on the ground, and shook her head at her own stupidity.

In truth, the lodge she was heading for (at least, she hoped she was heading in the right direction) wasn't far from the train station. Walking normally wouldn't have been a problem. She just hadn't factored in the earlier sunset this far north and the fact that it might be snowing.

Snowing, right before Christmas, in upstate New York? Not all that shocking.

Thankfully, her job scouting for a TV show meant she knew how to pack light—at least she wasn't dragging a suitcase behind her. She wore her bulky winter coat and boots, and everything else, including laptop, camera, and clothes, were in her backpack. She'd had to hike to sites before.

Just not in the damn snow.

The world held that silent quality that came only in the

winter. The snow padded the ground, muffled the air. All she could hear was her own breathing, and the occasional, tiny snap of a twig as some small animal settled for the night.

The birch trees' pale bark glowed in the moonlight.

Claudia felt like she stood in the middle of a snow globe.

She thought she'd walked the two miles already, but nary a house was in sight, not even a glow of lights. She didn't think the snow would have knocked out the power, so this was worrying. The GPS on her phone had been no help: the small dirt lanes didn't register on the map. And then, of course, because she'd spent too much time on the train working, her battery had died. She couldn't even call.

She was just about to turn around and head back to the station when she caught motion out of the corner of her eye. She hadn't heard anyone approach; her own gasp sounded loud against the sudden pounding of her heart.

Not a someone...a something. A large white dog—a husky or a white German shepherd, it was hard to tell in the dark—stood a few feet away, tail waving languidly, tongue out, watching her.

"Well, hello there, pup," she said in a soothing tone, holding out her hand flat. "Where did you come from?"

The dog barked, and jerked its head in a gesture that looked suspiciously like *Come on, then*. It took a few steps towards the trees, then looked back expectantly.

Its message was clear: *Follow me*.

Seriously?

The dog came back a few steps and barked again, this time more impatiently, then turned and looked over its shoulder.

The dog could be leading her to shelter, Claudia supposed. Or it could be leading her to someone or something in trouble. Or it could just be leading her...no, why would the dog be trying to lead her nowhere? Even if it wasn't to the lodge, it would be somewhere with a phone or a car. Dogs didn't lead people to scary shacks containing serial killers, after all.

Claudia always trusted her instincts, and they'd never proven her wrong. She also had a lot of faith in dogs. Her choice was clear.

She settled her pack more firmly on her shoulders and followed the dog into the woods.

The trees weren't closely spaced and there was no foliage beneath the snow to trip her up, although in a few open places the snow had piled up. The dog seemed to take delight in bounding off to leap through the drifts before running back to trot ahead of her.

They hadn't walked more than ten minutes when Claudia saw lights. As they drew closer, she breathed a sigh of relief, recognizing the stone-and-timber lodge from pictures. The dog had in fact led her directly to Heather Mountain Lodge.

The three-story building toed the line between Victorian and mountain rustic. The roof was steeply pitched to keep too much snow from collecting, with two levels of dormers and multiple chimneys dotting the expanse.

Warm lights glowed from multiple windows, bathing the snow in warm, welcoming gold, a gorgeous contrast to the midnight blue sky and gleaming snow. Fairy lights in the bare trees added to the cheer. Claudia felt warmer already.

Home. In an odd way, that's what it felt like, even though Claudia had never been here before. She'd grown up in the northeast, though, and the scene was familiar enough.

Plus, her tiny apartment—the tradeoff for a nice place in LA was size—had never felt homey, and now she'd been told that due to budget cuts, she was expected to telecommute.

She sighed, blowing out the melancholy. She'd worry about that after the holidays. Right now, she had a job to do.

"Good job, pup!" she said. The dog barked one more time and trotted away, around the building. Probably a doggie door in the back, leading to a mud room or kitchen.

She went up the flagstone steps to the enclosed porch that ran the length of the building and let herself in, stomping her feet on the entry rug to knock off the snow before continuing to the front door.

Before she could ring the bell, she saw movement through the glass, and then the door opened.

"You must be Claudia," the very attractive man said. His eyes were the same deep blue as the winter twilight she'd just hiked through, and his welcoming smile sparkled in those eyes like snow under moonlight.

Something tugged at her, deep in her core. It was like the sensation she'd felt when she'd seen the lodge. *Home.*

But that made no sense—tall-dark-and-handsome shouldn't evoke *home. Instant lust,* maybe (and there was that, too), but not *home.*

"Must I?" she asked cheekily, stepping inside.

"Mrs. Hawley said someone named Claudia was supposed to arrive tonight, and she's been fretting that you're late and your phone goes straight to voicemail," he said, his voice low and pleasant. He closed the door. "So it's a good assumption you're Claudia."

"Excellent powers of deduction," Claudia said, holding out her gloved hand.

"Excellent powers of being Claudia," he said, shaking her hand. "I'm Reese. D'you mind leaving your boots on the porch?"

She saw the row of winter footwear lined up next to a rough-hewn bench. Dropping her pack next to her, she sat to unlace her hiking boots.

She sensed, rather than saw, Reese lean comfortably against the doorjamb. A glance showed he'd tucked his hands in his pockets.

"Do you work here?" she asked.

"No. I was on my way back from the bathroom when I saw you on the porch. But I grew up nearby, so I'm familiar with the place."

She stood in her thick socks, and saw him grin. Thought she saw the flash of a dimple, even.

"And I figured," he went on, scooping up her pack for her, "here's my chance to meet this intriguing latecomer before anyone else. Good thing I trusted my instincts. Come on in," he added, stepping aside to let her enter. "Mrs. Hawley's in the parlor with some of the other guests."

It was warm inside, enough to make her chilled cheeks hurt in a pleasant way—although she had to admit it wasn't the only reason her cheeks were flushed. She shivered, adjusting to the change in temperature.

She followed Reese through the foyer, unable to decide whether to look at the gorgeous architecture or him (also gorgeous). The foyer, although paneled with dark wood, was welcoming thanks to the warm light from antique Tiffany lamps and the faded oriental rug covering the center of the floor. A steep staircase dominated the right side, its likely hand-carved newel posts a testament to an art form mostly lost today. The wood—currently wrapped with a sweet-smelling pine garland—shone, polished by more than a century of hands caressing the railing as residents and then hotel guests made their way up- or downstairs.

Claudia smiled, feeling the tension melt away. She already liked it here.

She had a job to do, so she shouldn't allow herself to be distracted by Reese, but unfortunately, she already was. Okay, maybe not full-on *attracted to* after their extremely brief conversation, but at least *appreciative of.*

The snug way his jeans hugged him didn't hurt, definitely. Nor did the in-need-of-a-trim black hair, striking blue eyes, and warm smile. Nor the comfortable way he led her through to the parlor. Not cocky, but simply confident, settled in his own skin.

She wouldn't have minded more time alone with him, but there were other people in the parlor, and that settled that.

"Oh goodness," said a tall, rangy older woman, "you must be Claudia."

"I must," she agreed this time. "You're Mrs. Hawley?"

"That I am." The woman's white hair framed a face that showed a lifetime of smiles in the fine lines around her eyes and mouth. "Let me show you to your room, dearie, and then you can settle in and meet folks. Shall I make you a pot of tea? Or hot chocolate? Or...?"

"Hot chocolate sounds lovely," Claudia said. She leaned in conspiratorially. "Especially if it has a nip of crème de menthe in it."

Mrs. Hawley smiled. "Absolutely," she said.

~

"THIS IS PERFECT," Claudia said when she saw her room. The turned-wood four-poster bed had a cream-colored, crocheted blanket at its foot and a lavender-scented sachet on the pillow, and the room's uneven wooden floors creaked as she entered. Cozy and charming. "I'll be down in a few minutes."

It took her even less than that—the lingering chill (although the room itself was toasty) drove her to drop her backpack and shuck her parka before plugging in her traitorous phone and heading downstairs to properly meet the rest of the guests.

Back in the parlor, she was happy to settle in an antique sofa near the stone fireplace, where a fire crackled and spat heat and the scent of wood smoke. Happy especially because the free spot was next to Reese.

"Mrs. Hawley's off making your hot chocolate; we had an early supper so she could let the cook go for the night because of the snow," Reese said. "Which doesn't bode well for breakfast."

"We aren't going to be snowed in for long, I hope?" asked a man wearing glasses and a Dr. Horrible T-shirt, who'd been introduced as Matt. He held hands with a pretty redhead—Holly—wearing multicolored striped socks and a matching crocheted hat.

"The weather report said it should stop snowing overnight," said a teenaged girl with a blond French braid, glancing up from her phone. Brittany, Claudia repeated to herself. Her parents, Tom and Sherry, had already gone upstairs, as had the final guest, Angela, a musician.

"And once the plow comes through, we'll be fine," Reese added.

Mrs. Hawley returned with Claudia's hot chocolate, and

now that this crop of guests was assembled, began her story.

"The White Lady," Mrs. Hawley said, settling herself into her chair and into her story. "We don't know much about who she was when she was alive, but we know this: She was married, and her husband was away one night in late December. I've heard different stories—that he'd been out hunting that day, that he went out in the storm to help someone. As the snow came down harder, she knew it would be more difficult for her husband to find his way home. So she went from window to window, lighting candles to guide him to safety."

Mrs. Hawley paused to take a sip of her own hot chocolate before continuing.

"Since then, each year, starting a day or two before Christmas and going until a day or two afterwards, after dusk falls she moves through the lower rooms of the house, lighting candles in the windows to bring her beloved home."

Holly shivered. "That's a beautiful story." She squeezed Matt's hand. "So romantic."

Romantic, yes, but whether there was any truth to the story...well, that was Claudia's job to figure out.

"What style of clothing does she wear?" she asked. "A nightgown? A Victorian dress? Earlier period, later?"

"Oh, well, I can't say for sure," Mrs. Hawley said, looking down at her hands. "I'm not an expert in these things."

"I understand," Claudia said. "It's just, if we can narrow down her clothing style, we can narrow down who she might be."

"Oh, that's right," Reese said, turning toward her in interest. Claudia felt that flutter in her stomach again at hearing his mellow voice. "You're from one of those reality shows—you're a ghost hunter."

Claudia laughed, glad that he seemed to be taking her seriously. "Not hardly. I'm a location scout; I don't get any air time at all. And *America's Legendary Ghosts* isn't a ghost-hunting show—we don't run around with EMF detectors or try to debunk the stories. We focus on the truth behind the legend...we want to know whether the ghost story has some basis in history. We're more of a history program than a reality show."

"So you're here to decide whether The White Lady is real or not?" Holly asked.

Claudia reluctantly turned her gaze away from Reese. "I'm here to discover whether there's any historical basis for The White Lady," she explained. Then, to Mrs. Hawley, she added, "I assume you've seen her?"

"Indeed I have." Mrs. Hawley sat up straight. "Every year."

"Please, tell me."

"We've had candles in the windows here in winter for as long as I can remember—and I've been here since I was a little girl. Even if no one sees her, people come down in the morning and find candles burning, or melted wax where the candles have burned down."

"And what happens if people try to interact with her?" Claudia asked.

"They can't," Mrs. Hawley said. "She doesn't respond to any attempts to communicate with her. If people come close, she disappears."

"Vanishes?" Claudia clarified.

"Essentially."

"Did her husband make it home?" Matt asked.

Mrs. Hawley looked sad. "We don't know," she said. "We just don't know."

"I'm guessing he didn't," Claudia said. "If he had, she wouldn't feel compelled to keep lighting the candles."

They all stared at her as if she'd just kicked their collective puppy. Clearly she'd harshed their mellow. What had they expected? Before she had a chance to speak, Brittany looked up from her phone and said, "Well, isn't it *obvious*? It's a *ghost*. It's not supposed to be *happy*."

Although the others nodded in agreement, that effectively killed the conversation. After one or two more half-hearted questions, the group broke up, Mrs. Hawley retiring for an early night so she could handle breakfast.

"You didn't get any supper, did you?" Reese asked Claudia.

She'd been so intent on learning about the ghost that she hadn't realized until now that she was starving, and she appreciated him realizing she might not have eaten. She had a power bar in her luggage, but the hell with that. Any extra time she could spend with him was a bonus, and if he could point her towards food....

"I had a snack on the train, but that was it," she said.

"Come with me."

She followed him to the kitchen—both because she didn't know where it was and because it was an opportunity to ogle his butt again in those faded, snug jeans.

The kitchen had been upgraded with professional appliances, but still held the sense of a homey Victorian kitchen, thanks to details such as herbs drying from a rack hanging from the ceiling, a fireplace with a bread oven along one wall, and an open wooden cabinet displaying blue-patterned china.

"You said you used to live here?" Claudia asked. "Mrs. Hawley seems comfortable with you."

"I grew up in the area," Reese said. He stripped off his sweater, and she caught a flash of taut abs dusted with dark hair as the T-shirt beneath rode up. Yummy. She fumbled herself onto a barstool, but he didn't notice, being too busy opening cabinets and pulling out a plate and bread with a comfortable ease, as if he were well acquainted with the layout. "My mom worked for Mrs. Hawley for a few years, so I hung out here a lot. I'd like to say I was helping, but I'm pretty sure I was just underfoot."

"I grew up in Albany, actually," Claudia said. "I've never been here, but I've been to Lake Placid a few times."

"Not too far away, then," Reese said. "Welcome back."

So different from the men she'd met in California, she mused. It wasn't that nobody was nice there, but she did work in Hollywood, after all. Everybody seemed to be angling for something—and seemed to be made of hard edges. Reese seemed confident, but in a comfortable way; like he was settled in his own skin.

Maybe that was the familiarity and comfort that tugged at her.

Claudia propped her elbows on the butcher block island. "So, have you seen The White Lady?"

"As a matter of fact, I have." He was leaning into the industrial refrigerator, so she couldn't see his face, although his deep voice was casual and self-assured. He didn't sound like he was lying. "I was walking by the parlor and I saw her in there. It scared the snot out of me, and I ran to find my mom."

He emerged from the fridge, balancing ham and cheese and condiments in his arms. Claudia held her breath until the food was safely deposited on the butcher block. She felt bad for not helping, but damn, she was tired.

"We moved the year after that," he went on. "Late summer. So I never had the chance to see her again."

"Is that why you've come back?"

He turned away to find a knife, turned back. "No, not really. I...my folks are both gone, and my brother and sister were off doing their own thing, so I just wanted to come back and recapture the fond memories." He handed her the knife and shoved the condiments across the island. "What about you? It must suck to work on Christmas."

She opened the jar of stone-ground mustard, spread some on the wheat bread. "Kinda. My family's big, and we decided a few years ago to make Thanksgiving the big holiday—my folks are in Florida now, and we rotate between locations—and we're on our own for Christmas."

More than *kinda*, she'd realized on the hike here, but she wanted to keep the conversation positive. No sense scaring a guy away by immediately admitting that you can't hold down a relationship because your job requires you to travel so much. Her last boyfriend finally up and decided that didn't work for him.

Oddly, it had worked for her. Oh, he hadn't been a bad guy—she thought she'd loved him, eaten an awful lot of Ben & Jerry's after his departure—but the fact was, she loved to travel and loved the chance to be on her own. Absence did make the heart grow fonder, at least for her.

Unfortunately, not many people shared that view, and constant travel made it hard to even get to know someone long enough to find out if they shared that view.

Claudia added ham, Swiss, and tomato slices to her sandwich, and continued focusing on the positive. "Being free on Christmas gives me a little more leeway—you'd be surprised how many ghost legends revolve around the holidays."

"Maybe Dickens was on to something."

She laughed. "Maybe so. There certainly haven't been any Thanksgiving ghosts for us." She put some baby spinach on the sandwich, covered it with a second slice of bread, and pressed down with both hands to smoosh it down to a more comfortable height. "I'm just glad I'm here this year. It's always depressing to be without snow on Christmas. Despite what the rest of Hollywood likes, I don't want to be wearing shorts in December. It's just *wrong*."

"I hear you," Reese said. "One year I was in Australia for Christmas. The big heavy Christmas dinner makes no sense when it's a bazillion degrees out." He was already tidying away the sandwich fixings.

"What took you there?" Claudia took a big bite of her sandwich, stifling a moan of pleasure. She hadn't realized she was *that* hungry. Maybe it was the crème de menthe talking.

"I'm a structural engineer, specializing in earthquake retrofits," he said. "I was working on a government contract."

Now that she had a little food in her (that wasn't sugar laced with alcohol), she was able to focus again. She found herself distracted by his hands, competently wiping down the butcher block.

Thought about those hands on her body.

She was tired, but she wasn't *that* tired.

"Does your job take you all over?" she asked, because dragging him down on the butcher block and having her way with him might be a tiny bit too forward.

"Everywhere there are earthquakes, which is as all over as you can get," he said.

"And where do you live when you're not wandering the globe?"

"I've got an apartment in the city, but it's mostly a place to store my stuff. I'm thinking about—"

They heard a shout, and then Holly appeared in the kitchen doorway. "Come quick!" she said. "We've seen The White Lady!"

Claudia dropped the second half of her sandwich and bolted for the foyer, Reese on her heels. When they arrived, the rest of the guests were there, in various stages of settling in: Angela was in a flowered flannel nightgown, with a matching robe belted firmly around her, while Tom's wet hair suggested he'd been in the shower.

"In the parlor, where we were earlier," Holly said.

Sure as shooting, the candles in the window had been lit, a smudge of wax on the windowsill indicating someone had bumped the candle after it had been burning.

"Candles," Claudia said. "Did anyone see The White Lady?"

"I did," Matt said, raising his hand. "I came back down to get my phone, and there she was. She vanished before I got into the room."

"Vanished how?" Claudia asked. She didn't want to sound suspicious; hated ruining the other guests' excitement. Even as she spoke, she felt the energy in the room drop.

"Just...I don't know, exactly." Matt looked abashed. "I turned to call up the stairs to Holly, and when I turned back, the Lady was gone. But I know she didn't go past me."

The parlor's only other door led to the dining room, and the door between the dining room and the kitchen had been open—surely she and Reese would have heard someone in there?

Claudia asked a few more questions, then decided not to investigate tonight. There would be time for that in the morning.

Time to figure out if this was a legend worth pursuing... and if Reese was, as well.

Nah. She'd already decided that he was. But exhaustion was crowding out interest, and she still had a job to do.

Dammit.

~

Claudia shoved the drapes aside and smiled at the sun sparkling on the fresh, untouched snow.

A good night's sleep under cozy flannel sheets and a warm down comforter had gone a long way to improving her outlook on life. The snow had been hauntingly lovely last night, but she'd been lost and cold and hungry; today, she could simply appreciate its beauty. She wondered how the dog was doing, and made a mental note to ask Mrs. Hawley.

The dining room had a big stone fireplace and large windows that looked out on the mountains. Quiet holiday music filled the background from unseen speakers.

Even better, the dining room had Reese in it.

And when she saw him, she had that same damn curious tug at her very core.

She said good morning to him, as well as Brittany, her parents, and Angela, who were the only other ones there, then helped herself to food from the sideboard. She slid into the seat catty-corner from Reese, wanting to watch him without being obvious. But from the way he smiled at her, she suspected he'd notice, because he'd be watching her, too.

His smile made her feel all melty, like an icicle in the sun. Damn, what was happening to her?

"This is just lovely," Sherry enthused. "I've always wanted to get away for Christmas. And I love the decorations."

"They're beautiful," Claudia agreed. "My apartment's way to small for a tree, and I travel so much that decorating seems more like clutter-adding than something festive."

Reese asked, "Well, then, what's your favorite part about Christmas?"

"Ideally, I love the ritual of it all," Claudia confessed. "Trimming the tree, wrapping the presents, sitting down for dinner with family..."

"And snow," Reese said with a wink that said he remembered their conversation from the night before. "Don't forget about the snow."

"But you can have the rituals without snow," Tom said.

Claudia had almost forgotten there were other people at the table.

"That's true," Reese said. "Claudia's right: It's about being with family and friends—rituals are about sharing the same joys with the people you love."

Everyone murmured assent, and then they all started discussing their rituals and childhood memories: tinsel versus garland, holly and mistletoe, favorite carols. And cookies. The cookie debate almost got a little heated.

Claudia, who didn't even like to bake, found herself wanting to make holiday cookies with Reese. Preferably with each of them wearing little more than an apron. He'd look adorable with flour on his nose. And wearing little more than an apron.

After breakfast, Reese asked, "What's your plan for today, ghost hunter?"

"Legend hunter, please," Claudia said, cradling her hands around her coffee mug. "I'm headed into town to meet with the county clerk to look at the lodge's records, and hit the local library for their archives."

He offered to drive her, and she happily took him up on it. She could have walked, but it wouldn't be a bad idea to make sure she knew the way first. Bonus: His truck had four-wheel drive and snow tires. The driveway had already been plowed, as had the lane, but it was still a bit slippery.

Claudia laughed at herself. The truth was, she was thrilled to have the opportunity to spend more time with him.

She hadn't even been here a day, and yet she was feeling something shifting, deep, like thick ice on a river just before it breaks free.

The drive reminded her to ask Mrs. Hawley about the dog. She hadn't seen it around today, so maybe it didn't live at the lodge, but at a nearby farm.

At the county courthouse, she waded through land and tax records, making photocopies of what she needed. By the time she was done, it was lunchtime, and she met Reese, who'd been running errands, at a local restaurant.

The proprietors had gone for a full-on log cabin feel, with exposed-log walls, a pot-bellied stove, deer heads on the wall, and a taxidermied black bear to greet her at the door.

Reese had arrived before her, and was already at a table with a steaming cup of coffee, his olive parka slung over the back of his chair. A second cup of coffee sat at her place.

"I remembered you had coffee this morning, but not what you put in it," he said, pushing creamer and sugar in her direction.

The gesture warmed her more than the heat inside the diner did.

His dark hair was mussed, either from having his hood up earlier or because he'd run his fingers through it. Either way, it worked on him, and Claudia wondered if it was soft, and how it would feel to run her own fingers through it. Then draw his face towards hers...

She turned her attention to the menu, made a random decision about food because she was thinking more about how Reese's lips would feel on hers, and put the menu back down.

She wasn't used to such instant attraction, not like this. She believed herself savvy enough to get a good sense of a person early on, but when it came to relationships, the process had always been gradual. *I like you, hm, maybe I'm interested, I wonder if...*

Physical attraction, sure. But this deeper tug, this feeling of things clicking into place?

Was it the holidays? The nostalgia for proper winter? Her dissatisfaction with the place she barely called home?

She realized Reese was watching her with those winter-twilight eyes, and answered her own questions. No, it wasn't any of those things. It was this. It was him, whether she was used to it or not.

"Everything okay?" he asked.

"Sorry," she said. "Wool-gathering." Then, before she could talk herself out of it, she added, "I'm...really glad we're able to have lunch together."

Oh, Claudia. So lame.

But he smiled and said, "Me, too. It's hard to have alone time in a house full of people, even in a house as big as the lodge."

The waitress came to take their order. When she left, the spell was momentarily broken.

"So what do you really think about The White Lady?" Reese asked after swallowing some coffee. "Is she real?"

"I want her to be," Claudia admitted. "But the bottom line for me—for my job—is whether the underlying legend is real. What about you? You saw her as a child—it wasn't a childish fantasy?"

"If she isn't real, I can't blame Mrs. Hawley for making her up," Reese said. "She's been a good source of tourism for the lodge even at other times of the year. But more than that, I believe Mrs. Hawley believes. Her own husband died of a heart attack—must be twenty years ago now—and I think she likes the idea of someone being able to guide her lover home."

"Oh." Claudia looked down at her paper placemat, which bore the history of the diner. "I didn't know that. How sad."

"Don't be sad." Reese put a hand over hers. "It was a long time ago, and I'm pretty sure she's had...friends since then. But she hasn't remarried, and I know the lodge is important to her, so..."

She caught her breath. Yes. She felt the solid, comforting warmth of his touch, felt the tug of *home*, and thought, *This. This is what I want when I stagger in after a long flight.*

And, *Well, this and a continuation of the touching until we've removed each other's clothes and...*

And, *Am I going crazy?* Her emotions were going haywire, attraction and longing and happiness and sadness ribboning together.

"I get that." Claudia gathered her feelings and her

thoughts. "It's just that so many of the stories are about loss. It just wears me down sometimes."

She'd never told anyone that before. She wasn't sure if she'd even realized it until now.

"I get that, too," Reese said. "We want to find our soulmates and have happy endings."

Claudia squinted at him, but he didn't sound like he was making fun of her. Quite the opposite, in fact: If anything, he looked wistful.

He went on. "My parents truly seemed to be happy with each other, really seemed to be in love. I guess I want to believe that's possible for anybody." He squeezed her hand, let go, and she felt an instant, sharp pang of loss.

Thankfully the waitress chose that moment to reappear with their lunches, giving her a distraction.

The cost was reasonable and the portions hearty—and, Claudia discovered, quite tasty. Her enormous bowl of chili had a nice bite to it, warming her after the walk over from the courthouse, and the buttered cornbread melted in her mouth.

"Enough about my job," she said after a few bites. "What about you?"

"It's hard, sometimes, going in after an earthquake to assess the damage and what can be done," he said. "But I like the fact that I can make buildings safer, prevent further destruction or injury. That part is truly satisfying. And I get to meet a lot of interesting people...for a little while, anyway."

"Same here," Claudia said. "But I'm also grateful for modern technology—I Skype with my folks every few weeks."

"My sister likes to call me while she's out walking," he

said. "Always multitasking. I Skype with my brother so I can see his kids—he's got three now."

"What about..." Claudia bit the bullet. "Anyone else?"

He shook his head. "No one special," he said. "It's hard to maintain a relationship given all the traveling I do."

"This probably sounds weird," he said, "and may be blowing my chances, but...I don't need to be around someone twenty-four/seven. I like having time away. Then when I'm with someone, I'm really *with* them, not taking them or our time together for granted." He gave a half-shrug, a gesture so small she almost missed it. "I know it's unusual—I've met some pretty independent women who just didn't want that level of independence."

"Tell me about it," Claudia said. "That's why my last relationship tanked. I love my job, and everywhere it takes me, but finding someone else who understands that love..."

Suddenly self-conscious, she looked down at her half-eaten chili in the white porcelain bowl.

Reese cleared his throat, and to her relief, changed the subject. "How did you end up at the show?" he asked.

She smiled, grateful for the reprieve. "I sort of fell into it. I was the family genealogist, and I played around with cameras, and couldn't decide what to major in at college. Eventually I moved to LA with a friend who wanted to be an actress, and got a job as a PA, and...I'm good at research."

"It's a good thing to be good at," he said.

"Yeah, although my boss just realized I could be good at it anywhere," she said, and proceeded to tell him about being forced to telecommute and loathing her tiny apartment. "Of course," she concluded, "I could always just become impossibly hipster and work in coffee shops."

"I rank airports by whether or not they have free wireless and how many available outlets there are," Reese said, his mouth curving into an impossibly cute grin.

"Ditto the planes themselves," Claudia said. "Give me power at my seat and I'll fly you forever."

"And hotel rooms," Reese said, almost at the same time. "Wireless, outlets, comfortable bed..."

"Absolutely," Claudia said, thinking about comfortable beds and Reese and room service.

Their shared laughter made her feel so light and airy, like a snowflake in a swirl of wind.

Despite the local library being in a modern building, the older records hadn't been updated to the modern age, leaving Claudia to slog through ancient microfiches of local newspaper archives and census records in the chilly, damp windowless basement.

Still, there was something about this kind of research she loved; the chance uncovering of a mystery, the allure of discovering a treasure of information.

To her delight, Reese had come with her, and helped her by making photocopies and bringing her books on local history.

It was already dusk by the time they left, Claudia's bag stuffed full of paperwork to review over the next two days.

Everyone seemed in good spirits at dinner, and hopeful that the ghost would make another sighting. She liked the way Reese was easy with everyone, even drawing Brittany away from her phone for a conversation about technology.

Plus the venison stew, roasted vegetables, and an apple pie with locally made maple ice cream almost sent Claudia into a food coma.

Afterwards they repaired to the parlor again. Reese made a point of sitting next to Claudia on the sofa, stretching out his long, jean-clad legs towards the fire.

While the other guests played a game or read and Mrs. Hawley knitted, Claudia started in on the reams of photocopies. This was a work trip—she wasn't really on vacation, despite the holiday—but when she curled up Indian-style, her knee bumping Reese's thigh, he smiled, and so she left it there, enjoying the contact. Even if it was a distraction.

Especially if it was a distraction.

This time, it was Angela who spotted something moving in the dining room when she stood to stoke the fire. Once again, they rushed across the foyer into the other room.

"What was that?" Tom asked, and at the same time Holly said "Was that a light outside?" and Claudia had to admit that really did look like the flicker of candle flame outside the window, although neither she nor the rest of them clearly saw a person.

"We should go check for footprints," she suggested.

Clouds obscured the stars and moon, but the ambient light from the lodge along with the flashlights Mrs. Hawley procured for them provided enough illumination to show that there were no footprints outside the dining room.

It was Brittany who spotted the white candle in the white snow, its wick blackened, showing it had been used.

They all trooped back inside, kicking snow off their boots on the porch and shivering in the warmth. Mrs. Hawley went off to make hot chocolate and hot buttered rums.

Reese waited until the others had gone and just he and Claudia were still on the porch. After the flurry of other people, it felt good to be alone with him, if only for a few moments. The light gleaming from inside haloed his dark hair in its usual messy state, and she fought the urge to tame it just so she could feel it.

"What do you think about it?" he asked.

She gave a cautious shrug, glad that she had someone she felt she could trust to bounce ideas off of. "I have to admit I saw *something*, but I can't swear it was candlelight. Finding the candle on the ground was…an interesting development, though."

"And how's the research going?"

"Nothing to confirm or deny yet, but the night is young," she said. "Mrs. Hawley gave me a book on Adirondack ghost stories that includes the legend of The White Lady…but the account was given by her father, who bought the lodge before Mrs. Hawley was born. I'm still tracing back the property records from then. I need to either find some kind of proof of a woman whose husband died around the holidays, or a very old account of the ghost, or even both." She tucked her boots beneath the bench and stood.

"No rest for the wicked?" he asked.

She laughed. "Maybe tomorrow, if I get enough work done."

"Is there anything I can do to help?" he asked, holding the door to the lodge open for her.

"I wouldn't take you away from *your* vacation, but no, at this point it's all research I need to do." She smiled, honestly feeling her next words. "But I really appreciate it."

Dammit. Why couldn't this research trip be longer? She wanted more time with him.

Maybe they'd get a blizzard and get snowed in, and they could hole up in one of their bedrooms and have Mrs. Hawley send up the dog with food like a St. Bernard…

~

IT DID SNOW the next day, although the flakes drifted down languidly, showing no interest in being collectively labeled a blizzard. Clearly they hadn't gotten the memo.

Still, it made Claudia's work all the more pleasant. She'd missed the feeling of curling up in a comfy sweater and thick socks by a warm fire, watching the snow outside while she read and made notes and cross-referenced things.

The room smelled of pine from the garlands and cinnamon from the arrangement on the birch side table, where a lamp with amber and glass shades shaped like calla lilies illuminated her reading.

The rest of the guests had gone out cross-country skiing, so she had the place to herself, except for the cook making their supper feast and Mrs. Hawley catching up on paperwork in her own office.

Reese had sat with her after lunch, catching up on e-mail on his tablet. When he left with the others, he said it was to give her time to work. But the fact was, she'd been fine having him in the room. He'd respected her by staying quiet, and when she'd tossed a fact or idea at him, he'd had helpful comments.

No, she hadn't been just fine. She'd liked having him there. More than she'd expected.

The thought made her smile, kept her warm while she read and researched, stayed with her as the midnight blue of twilight fell. She poured a Scotch on the rocks and stood by the window, watching the blue-white glow of the snow and the flakes trickling down past the icicles hanging from the eaves.

She intended to curl back up with her research, but

instead she picked up the brochures she'd seen on a side table, flyers listing local homes for sale.

She sat down, spread them out on the sofa, picked up each one. The pictures showed the houses in all seasons—the area was known for skiing, both downhill and cross-country, snow shoeing, ice skating, and even dogsled rides on the frozen lake. In the summer, there was hiking, swimming, boating.

She was surprised at how they made her heart wrench, just a little. What was it about a chalet-style cottage, its roof steeply pitched to slough off snow, that was just so damned charming?

In truth, she'd barely had a few sips of whiskey before she closed her eyes. Resting her head against a pillow, she listened to the soft music playing from hidden speakers: a chorale version of "Silent Night."

She thought about saving her money and buying a holiday home in the mountains.

She thought about Reese.

And smiled.

Claudia didn't think she'd fallen asleep—she'd been only drifting—but something started her into full consciousness. She blinked, clearing her head and her vision.

Full dark had fallen; the only illumination in the room was from the lily lamp beside her...

...and a white taper candle in a simple pewter holder, burning in the window.

She sat bolt upright, looked around. At the edge of her sight she saw movement, a flash of white, in a shadowed corner of the room—but when she turned, it disappeared.

The hell?

Her heart pounding, she skirted the sofa and occasional

table and a plant stand to get to the corner, where an interior wall met an outer wall, near where she'd stood to look out the window earlier.

Nothing there but paneled walls of stained fir. She reached out a hand...

And suddenly the room was filled with light.

Claudia *eeped* and spun, only to dissolve into relieved laughter when she saw Reese in the doorway, his hand at the push-button light switch.

"You startled me!" she said, her hand on her chest. If she'd thought her heart was pounding before...holy moly.

But now her heart was pounding for a different reason.

"There's a candle," he said. It would have been a non sequitur under any other circumstances.

"I fell asleep," she said as he walked towards her, which made her heart do a little kathump in between the thuds. She was glad he was back—which didn't surprise her. "I woke up and the candle was there and then I thought I saw something in this corner, but..." She lifted her shoulders in a shrug. "I got nothin'."

"Huh," he said. He cocked his head, his shaggy black hair flowing with the movement. "That's interesting."

"Why?"

"Tom and Sherry weren't ready to leave earlier, so I went outside to look at the house from a different angle. I don't have the blueprints for the house, obviously, but the measurements I took don't quite seem to add up."

"How so?" Claudia asked.

"As near as I can tell, this room ought to be wider than it is, given the placement of the windows here in the parlor and in the smoking room," he said.

Right—he was a structural engineer. He'd notice things like that. But it wasn't just about him being an engineer; he noticed details, filed them away. Like her coffee at the diner. It was part of his competence, that quiet intelligence, and she admired it.

It was her turn to cock her head. "You don't think it's just a factor of the house being added on to over the years?"

"I don't think so—both rooms are, as near as I can tell, part of the original building."

"Huh," Claudia said. "What does that mean?"

"Let find out," he said, and started tapping on the wooden panels.

"Oh, come on," she said. "It's not like we're in an episode of *Scooby-D*—wait, go back. Does that one sound different to you?"

He went back and rapped again on one of the rectangular panels. "It does—more hollow."

He felt around the panel, and Claudia could see that it was loose. Not a huge surprise in a house this old...the surprise was when he pressed against it and slid it sideways, revealing a dark hole.

Every bad horror movie raced through her head as Reese stuck his hand in the rectangular opening and felt around. A moment later he said, "I think I feel a latch."

Another moment, and a section of the wall swung inward, just wide enough for a not-too-large person to slip through. If the parlor weren't well lit, it would be hard to see the dark opening unless you were looking for it.

She leaned in and caught the scent of tallow. Besides, that, though, the room—or passage—didn't smell musty or unused. No cobwebs, not much dust. The space was narrow and long; the light didn't extend to the other end, but she was pretty sure there'd be another secret door leading to another room.

"You know," she said, turning to Reese, "I read something that said the Underground Railroad was active in and around Heather Mountain. John Brown's Farm is nearby."

"That makes a lot of sense," he said. "So, what are we going to do? It seems to me we've solved the mystery of The White Lady."

"I think I need to talk to Mrs. Hawley," she said.

"It's Christmas Eve," he reminded her, the blue of his eyes dark and grave.

"I know," she said, glad that he cared. "I'm not going to expose her—again, it doesn't matter to me whether the ghost is real or not. But I do need to find out the truth."

"I'd like to be there when you do," he said.

"I was planning on it," she said, and took his hand. It was, she realized, only the second time they'd held hands (the gloved handshake when they'd first met didn't count). It felt natural, as if they'd been doing it for a long time—as if they fit. His fingers twined with hers.

"It doesn't mean," he said softly, "that there isn't a happy ending."

Claudia had a feeling he wasn't just talking about the ghost.

"Let's find out," she said. She wasn't just talking about the ghost, either.

This wasn't something she wanted to do, but having Reese by her side made it easier. And just seemed right.

Mrs. Hawley's office was a back porch that had been converted into an interior room when additions had been made to the main house. Access was through the kitchen, and the smell of roasting turkey and sautéed onions made Claudia's mouth water.

A built-in desk took up much of one wall of the long, narrow room. Unlike the rest of the lodge, which was kept in an artfully cluttered but neat Victorian style, here papers and notebooks were scattered and piled along with office supplies, a glass doorknob, and three coffee cups. On the wall were framed pictures of who Claudia assumed were Mrs. Hawley's children and grandchildren.

"Well, hello, you two," Mrs. Hawley said, closing her laptop with a snick. "What...oh dear. I can tell by your expressions something is wrong."

Claudia looked at Reese. "Not wrong, exactly," she said, and then told Mrs. Hawley that they'd found the passageway.

The older woman's shoulders slumped. "You're right," she said. "We're almost positive the passageway was a hiding place for runaway slaves. It ends in the pantry, and from there you can get down into the root cellar, which has outside access."

"And The White Lady?" Claudia had to ask.

"It's possible—probable—that my father made her up, as a way to advertise the lodge. I kept up the ruse."

"With help, I'm guessing," Reese said.

Mrs. Hawley looked down at her hands. They were strong, sturdy, and Claudia saw she still wore her wedding ring, a plain white-gold band. "Yes," she admitted. "My son's an electrical engineer; he rigged some small effects. And I hire a girl to pose as the ghost at Christmastime, although sometimes I do it, too." She stood, looked at both of them. "You're not going to tell, are you?"

"It's Christmas Eve," Reese said. "That wouldn't be in the spirit of things."

"There's no reason to expose The White Lady as a fraud," Claudia said. "It does mean we can't feature the lodge on the show, but if the legend brings in customers, keep doing what you're doing."

"Thank you," Mrs. Hawley said with heartfelt emotion.

"You know," Claudia said, struck by inspiration, "you could come up with an even better legend about the passage and the Railroad. The ghost could be year-round, lighting a candle to let the Underground Railroad know when it's safe to come. I'm sure you could find some historical accounts to back up the story—which might make you eligible for the show. I'd be willing to help you with the research."

She didn't really have the time to do that—even while she'd been working here, she'd been doing preliminary research for three other possible show topics—but she'd grown fond of the Heather Mountain Lodge in the short time she'd been here.

Back in the parlor, looking at the decorated tree, its white lights glittering, she said to Reese, "I wish I could just grab all this and...I don't know, stop time for a little while." She laughed, swirling the last dregs of her whiskey in the glass. "I wish I could just live here."

"I was thinking the same thing," Reese said, and she looked up, startled. He picked up the brochures she'd left on the sofa. "In fact, I was looking at houses, somewhere to come on my time off. Maybe you should, too."

Claudia stared at him. *Tug. Click.* It didn't just make logical sense. It made *emotional* sense. She could live anywhere, and what were wishes but things to make real, if you really wanted them?

She always trusted her instincts.

She raised her glass. "And we should make a pact to meet here every Christmas?"

He smiled, but those midnight blue eyes held a hint of

seriousness. "No," he said, and before the wave of disappointment could crash over her, he added, "I wouldn't want to wait that long, would you?"

Her breath caught in her throat. She'd been half-joking, not realizing how much, until this very moment, she wanted him to say something like that.

"No, I don't think I would," she said.

Now the smile reached his eyes, made them flash in the glow of the tree's lights.

There was more here, Claudia knew, than Christmas magic. Like spring waiting under the cover of snow. That's the reason people brought in trees and decked the halls with greenery: to remind them, through the long winter darkness, that the sun would return and the earth would be abundant again. She'd half-forgotten that, missing the seasons in southern California.

There were so many questions to ask and answer, but not at this moment, she decided—it was Christmas Eve. Not a time for worries or fretting about the future. A time for rejoicing in the moment.

She didn't let Reese draw her in for a kiss—she met him halfway. Finally got to indulge the feel of his hair beneath her fingertips as their lips met and the world around them swirled like snow in a snow globe, and she thought she could stay here forever in the magic. It was only when laughter and voices echoed in the foyer that they pulled apart, but not before Reese caressed her cheek and said, "Now, tell me you'd want to wait until next Christmas to do that again."

"Not on your life," she said.

Dinner was full of laughter and talking, exactly how Claudia loved it, with everyone telling stories of their day (except all Claudia said was that she'd just missed seeing the ghost, drat it all). Afterwards, there were carols around the piano—much to her surprise, Reese played. A man of many talents; she liked that.

When they went upstairs, he stopped by her door. He took her hands in his and squeezed them gently. "Sleep tight," he said.

As earlier, she didn't stop to think, didn't know she'd made a decision until she said "Oh, don't be ridiculous," untangled her fingers from his, and reached up to draw him down for as toe-curling a kiss as she could muster.

At least, it curled *her* toes. At some point, it stopped being something she was trying to do and became something they were sharing.

When they drew apart, she asked a question with her eyes, and he answered. She took him by the hand again, and led him into her room.

IT WAS ALWAYS STRANGE, Claudia mused, when you felt entirely different—in this case, high on the giddy, bubbling joy—and nobody else seemed to notice except the person you shared it with. And except for Brittany, who walked by them and pointed meaningfully at the mistletoe they happened to be standing under.

When they kissed, they thought they heard a low, satisfied laugh, but when they broke apart, Brittany was already in the dining room, and nobody else was near.

After breakfast, they all repaired once again to the parlor. There was a new off-white candle on the windowsill, mostly burned down. Claudia glanced at the corner and smiled.

After yesterday's snowfall, the sun had come out again,

glazing the snow with a brilliance almost too bright to look at. It glinted off the icicles hanging from the eaves, and turned the snow on the trees to glittering fairy dust.

Mrs. Hawley had presents for all of them: small frames of heather pressed under glass. Matt and Holly had brought handmade bookmarks for everyone; Tom and Sherry passed out little carved bear and deer that they'd picked up at a gift shop in town; and Angela gave everyone CDs of a friend's music.

Claudia gave everyone locally made maple syrup, and Reese had had a similar idea, presenting boxes of maple candy shaped like maple leaves and pine cones, so sweet it made your teeth ache.

But Reese had another present for Claudia, which he gave her after everyone had gone off to tromp in the snow.

The box was only about six inches square, so she was unprepared for the weight of it.

She tugged off the curled blue ribbon; tore off the wrapping paper, white with blue snowflakes; opened the plain box.

"Ohhh..."

She shook the snow globe, watching the tiny white flakes swirl and dance around a winter forest scene and a building that looked much like Heather Mountain Lodge.

He must have bought it that first day, when they'd gone into town so she could do her research. That made it even more special.

"A little piece of the Adirondacks to take home to California," Reese said. "And snow to get you through the warm winter."

"It's perfect," Claudia said, her voice catching. "Thank you."

And she realized, yes, snow to get her through the winter. But not winter in LA, not ever again.

He held out his hand, helped her to her feet. "Speaking of snow," he said, "let's go outside and enjoy it. I'm thinking there's a potential snowman with our names on it."

~

INSTEAD, they went for a walk in the woods.

Snow clung to the branches and covered the ground, pristine. There were no signs of her footprints or of the big white dog's paw prints from just a few nights before.

Claudia's gloved hand curled around Reese's, comfortable, strangely familiar, and ever-exciting.

"I've been thinking," Reese said.

"Hm?"

"You want to move here, I want to move here, and I think, given everything, that we might as well skip a step and look at buying one house, not two, and moving here."

"You're not just...being logical, are you?" Claudia asked, because she had to be sure, had to hear him say it. "As in, we're rarely home, so why not be roommates and share a house?"

He shook his head, slowly, as he gathered her up in his arms. "No," he said. "I'm talking about *sharing* a house, and *sharing* a future."

He kissed the tip of her nose, his lips warm against her chilled flesh, then moved in for a long, slow kiss that warmed her all over.

And that was exactly how she'd hoped he'd respond.

~

THE SUN DIDN'T LAST; by the next morning, clouds had muted the sky again, heavy with potential snow. Fitting, Claudia thought, that she should leave in the weather she arrived in.

"Thank you so much," Claudia said sincerely, taking Mrs. Hawley's hands between hers. She'd already reiterated her willingness to help research the lodge's connection to the Underground Railroad. "It's beautiful here, and that's because of your hospitality and love for the lodge. From the staff, to the stories...even the dog that helped me find my way here."

Beside her, she sensed Reese suddenly going still. Mrs. Hawley cocked her head.

"Dog? What dog? I don't know what you mean."

"I've been meaning to ask you about him. A big white dog, in the woods the day I arrived. It led me here, through the snow. I was lost..." She trailed off at Mrs. Hawley's confused expression.

"I haven't got a dog," the older woman said. "I don't even know anyone around here who has a big white dog." Then she looked at Reese. "Didn't you have a big white dog when you were a boy?"

Reese's face was a blank mask. "Yes. Albus."

"That's it, Albus," Mrs. Hawley said. "A sweet dog, that one."

"Well," Claudia said, trying to recover, "if you see another big white dog in the area, thank it for me. And thank you again."

Reese didn't say anything as she shouldered her pack and followed him out to his truck. Her breath misted in the air as she climbed in, dropped the pack at her feet. He turned up the heat, but it took a few minutes for the blowing air to shift from cold to warm, and by that time they were down the driveway.

The truck bumped along the lane. Why were trucks always louder than cars inside? She'd arrived in silence, and was leaving in sound, and while in many ways she preferred the silence, she didn't like not hearing Reese's voice.

He'd pulled in on himself, and she wasn't sure if he was angry, or didn't believe her about the dog, or if he'd done a one-eighty and decided they'd moved too fast.

Hell, what had *she* been thinking, falling in love with a guy she'd barely just met?

Trust your instincts. Somehow, she didn't feel worried.

Her instincts told her to give him time.

They arrived at the station, parked in the tiny lot, which was mostly empty except for two other cars, one of which was half-covered with snow. The station itself was small, too, just a white clapboard building with a black "witch's hat" roof, steeply pointed but still covered with snow, and an additional covered waiting area with the same type of roof.

Claudia reached for the door handle, but stopped before she opened the door. Reese had shut off the truck but made no move to open his door, and even though he was just dropping her off and didn't need to come with her, something stayed her hand. Intuition, again.

He finally spoke. "Tell me about the dog," he said, looking at the slowly fogging windshield instead of her.

So she told him about being lost, and the dog coming out of the woods, and then leading her to the lodge before bounding off behind it. "Why?" she finished.

"Like Mrs. Hawley said, when I lived here as a kid, I had a White German Shepherd. One time I was walking home and the snow was so thick I lost my sense of direction, and he found me and led me home through the woods." He finally turned and looked at her, blue eyes intent. "I've never told anyone that. Not even Mrs. Hawley."

"Well," Claudia said, feeling a curious sense of warmth, like something melting beneath her breastbone, "perhaps that means we've found the ghost after all. I believe, truly, that it was Albus who found me and led me to the lodge."

A slow smile touched Reese's lips. "I believe that, too. He had good instincts, Albus did."

"Who knows," Claudia said, "maybe he's been doing it for years."

"Or maybe he just helps people I'm supposed to meet. People who...are meant to be in my life."

Claudia's heart thumped, and she smiled, too, at that. "Then I have even more reason to be grateful." Reluctantly, she added, "My train should be here any minute now."

"Then let's go," Reese said.

She exited the truck, the cold briefly sucking the air out of her lungs. She supposed if she lived here all the time, she might complain, but right now it felt exhilarating. She heaved her pack onto her shoulders, and Reese walked with her. They were the only ones there.

The snow began drifting down, fat, languid, dancing flakes.

Once they were on the wooden platform, he turned to her and said, "I have some time off in January after I finish my current project. I could come to LA...."

Claudia felt a warm flicker in her chest, like a growing flame. "I have a better idea," she said. "I'll put in for vacation time, too, and we'll meet back here."

"Have a proper stay at the lodge?" Reese's mouth quirked in a grin.

"Snuggle under the covers and look at property listings."

"I think I can distract you away from those...."

"Challenge accepted," she said.

In the distance came the faint whistle of a train, mournful and yet expectant, inviting her to another adventure. It reminded her that she loved to travel, even if she didn't want to leave just yet.

Reese cradled her face in his hands, bent to kiss her again.

With the snow swirling around them, she felt again as if they were in their own snow globe, the world existing only for the two of them, the moment locked in time.

And she knew she had a new holiday ritual, one she'd start as of next year, in their house.

She'd leave a candle burning in the window.

She knew Reese would understand.

THE REAL
HOUSEWITCHES OF
CALAFIA COUNTY

I'd had my mani-pedi done to both celebrate the upcoming holiday and my own backyard: blue that matched the infinity pool and white for the marble columns that held up the lanai roof. My high-heeled sandals clicked on the painted concrete as I set out glasses, an ice bucket, and a pitcher of jalapeño-lime margaritas. As well as the bottle of white rum, because Felisha often preferred it on the rocks with a twist of lime.

A few simple appetizers: Dates stuffed with goat cheese and wrapped in bacon. Crostini with bruschetta made with tomatoes from my own garden. A vegan white bean and artichoke dip with organic chia seed crackers.

It was a balmy seventy-two degrees, without a cloud in the sky. The city view over the valley with the mountains beyond was exquisite as always.

Winter Solstice in Southern California was approaching, and my fellow coven members and I had planning to do.

I was new to the West Coast, new to the neighborhood, new to the group. My husband was making the transition from producing Broadway plays to producing movies, and the differences between NYC and Hollywood were monumental in some ways, minor in others.

Being welcomed into the gated community coven made things easier. I still wanted our get-together to be perfect, though.

The front doorbell chimed, and although the door was unlocked (gated community and all), I still went to answer it.

Vanessa was the first to arrive, as usual. She wore her dark hair up off her neck in a fancy French twist. Her red one-piece bathing suit highlighted her light brown skin and her fake eyelashes highlighted her big dark eyes. Khaki shorts and sandals completed her outfit.

We hugged and air-kissed, even though we'd seen each other earlier that day at spin class.

(Hey, magic can't fix everything, not without consequences. A little glamour is one thing. Hard work at the gym and maybe the occasional nip-and-tuck are required to maintain oneself, witch or no.)

"Come on back," I said. "The others will be here soon."

She adjusted her red leather bag (which matched her suit) on her shoulder. Despite her careful makeup, I could see the dark circles under her eyes, and I could feel her unsettled aura as if she were throwing it at me.

"You need a margarita," I said.

"Goddess, yes!"

I'd just poured her one when the other two arrived.

Felisha, with her mahogany skin, nearly poreless (and that was natural, damn her). She looks like an Egyptian goddess, and unsurprisingly favored those deities in her personal work.

Shay, with her pale skin and long, curly red hair,

looking like a Pre-Raphaelite goddess. She bucked fashion (gasp!) by wearing long, flowing skirts, tea-stained lace and pale silks, and floaty scarves (although she ditched the latter when she was working on her jewelry, because trailing scarves tended to scatter beads and catch fire from the soldering iron).

"You'll never believe what she did this time!"

We didn't need to ask who Shay was talking about. We knew: Anastacia, the president of our Home Owner's Association.

Anastacia and her husband had been among the first residents of the community. Her husband had been the hereditary witch and had been influential in forming a neighborhood for our kind. Anastacia had been supportive of him, but she really didn't know as much about us. He'd died years ago and Anastacia, well, she'd been on the HoA board all along, arguing that she'd earned the position.

Shay waved a piece of paper. "She wrote me up for not taking my Samhain decorations down within, and I quote, 'the proscribed time period'."

Felisha frowned. "I don't remember you still having Samhain decorations up."

"Exactly! The besom"—Shay was referring to a witch's ritual handmade broom—"by the front door is something I always display, no matter the season. But she wouldn't budge. I still have to pay her ridiculous fine."

"Okay, why don't you sit down and I'll get you a drink?" I said, leading her to one of the overstuffed white sofas in the outdoor living space by the pool. Vanessa took the cue and dipped a glass in purifying salt before pouring in the margarita mix and garnishing it with a lime.

When Shay gets worked up, she sets things on fire. It's not her fault; fire is her element and passion runs in her veins. But this is Southern California, and the last thing anyone needed was an errant spark that set off a forest fire.

Combined, we likely had the power to put out the fire before it spread, but who wants to take that chance?

Shay took a hefty sip of the margarita, closed her eyes, and sighed. I felt the worst of the energy flow out of her, dissipating into the air. I flicked my fingers, dispersing it further so it didn't land on an unsuspecting passer-by.

"An it harm non, honey," I said, quoting the Wiccan rede. "An it harm none."

"It's a minor thing in the long run, I know," she said, "but Lord and Lady, she irks me. With the problems I'm having making jewelry, I don't have a lot of extra cash to deal with her petty fines."

Shay designed high-end jewelry, both for the masses and for the pagan community. The pagan jewelry was where she made the bulk of her money, because she imbued each piece with magic depending on what the wearer needed. She had the ability to know what each piece required, and then she could market it accordingly.

But she'd hit early menopause, and the energy surges and hot flashes were seriously dicking with her spellwork.

Imagine trying to film a movie when the generator keeps blowing.

We were all on edge this year, each with something to work through.

Vanessa's ex-husband died in November, and even though he was her ex (cheating, embezzling from his own company), she still had complicated feelings about him, and she wasn't handling his death well. Felisha was dealing with empty nest syndrome and worrying too much about her kids. As for me...

I was the only one without a real problem, honestly. My

issues were small beans compared to theirs. I was just... between projects. At loose ends.

I know most people look at us in our cushy gated community and assume we're trophy wives of rich husbands (sometimes true) or living off fat divorces (also sometimes true) who do nothing all day but shop and gossip and have spa days (occasionally true as well). All of that probably describes the *Real Housewives* shows on TV. (I haven't seen them.)

But as witches, along with harming none, we have a responsibility to the world. To nature, to energy, to balance. So we all try to find ways to make the universe a better place.

One of my talents is organization. I mean, I'm scary-good at it. I either go into an existing charity and get them on track, or I start a new one and get it running smoothly... at which point I get bored and move on.

Oh, of course I was helping out with the Winter Solstice ritual, but the girls had it running well already so it wasn't much of a challenge. They also host an associated gala fundraiser for a different charity each year.

But in terms of a new, big project to whip into shape and make run like clockwork? I had nada. Nothing.

The Solstice ritual was going to be in part to bring Vanessa closure, Felisha peace, Shay focus, me clarity and direction. The theme of dark into light worked for everyone.

And nobody, not even Anastacia, was going to dick with us, by the Goddess.

Of course, I didn't expect a notice from the HoA to appear the next morning on *my* kitchen island, either.

I was brewing a cup of sustainable Costa Rican roast and reviewing the instructions our cook had left for us. Because I wasn't yet working full-time, we employed him only three days a week, but he prepped meals for the other nights so all I had to do was assemble and pop things in the oven, essentially.

Or toss enormous salads, which seemed to be a local thing.

Which was a good thing, because unlike most hedge-witches, I didn't have the innate drying-herbs-and-candle-making abilities. Anything more than assembling hors d'oeuvres and mixing drinks was beyond me.

Our kitchen—bigger than my first apartment—is done in tasteful shades of gray. Pale gray granite shot through with darker streaks, stainless steel appliances, and round pendant lamps with round, clear bulbs exposing the filaments.

The room smells of herbs—just because I can't grow them doesn't mean my friends can't donate them—and sunshine from the four high folding doors that lead to an outdoor eating patio.

The HoA notice probably shouldn't have surprised me. After all, we'd received a fine on our very first day, for having our garage door open for more than, oh, one-point-two seconds.

On our first day, when we were *moving in* and the movers needed *access* to the *garage and shit*.

We paid the fine because at that point, we didn't want to rock the boat.

This boat was gonna capsize pretty damn soon.

There was a popping sound like a light bulb blowing out, the briefest odor like a struck match, and the HoA notice was floating down from a spot about a foot above the kitchen island.

My heather-gray, handle-less coffee mug cradled between my palms, I watched, stunned, as the paper settled gently on the island before I could rouse myself to pick it up.

You've got to be kidding me. What now?

I flicked a finger, drawing the paper to me.

According to bylaw number blah de blah, outside rituals of more than three attendees had to be pre-approved by the board.

At first I thought the notice was referring to the Solstice ritual, but why had it come to me when I wasn't in charge.

Then I realized: it was referring to our *meeting* yesterday.

I set down my mug. Carefully. Took a deep breath in through my nose, out through my mouth, grounding.

When I felt centered and calm (mostly calm) again, I called Anastacia.

Even though she'd just sent the notice, I had to leave a message, although she called me back a few moments later. "Hello dear!" she said. She called everyone *dear*. As if that was going to make anyone less cranky. "What can I do for you?

"It's about this notice I just received."

"Which notice is that, dear?"

Another calming breath. I quoted the bylaw number and rule.

"Oh, *that*," she said as if it were nothing. I imagined her waving a hand dismissively. She was the type who wore multiple chunky gold and diamond rings, all gifts from her late husband.

I waited for her to continue, but she didn't.

"It wasn't a ritual," I said finally. "It was a meeting of the Solstice ritual and fundraising committee."

I supposed she could argue that hors d'oeuvres and margaritas were akin to cakes and ale, but...

The real issue was that somehow, she or one of her cronies had looked into my backyard. My private backyard. My backyard that wasn't visible unless you went through a gate and then stood on a box to peer over a wall. Or you used a drone. Or some magical means I didn't even want to think about right now.

"Oh!" Anastacia said. "Sorry about that, dear. Just fill out the appropriate form and turn it in to the board, and we'll review it and reverse the decision."

"A form," I said.

"Yes, it's in the appendix of the bylaws."

As we'd been talking, I'd been heading to my home office. I hadn't done much with the space since we moved in because I hadn't had any good projects to work on. The walls were a soothing sage green and the trim was white. An ergonomic chair and L-shaped mahogany desk looked toward the French doors that led to the rest of the house, with a matching vertical file cabinet against a wall. No knickknacks yet, although a sage bundle sat in a clam shell on the filing cabinet, left over from when I'd smudged the room to purify it.

I jiggled the mouse to wake up my computer screen, and asked, "Are the bylaws online?" I assumed I could fill out the form that way.

"Oh, I'm afraid not. Just one of those things we haven't gotten around to yet." She laughed. I didn't.

"Can I drop by and pick up a copy, then?" Sending me the entire bylaws the same way she'd sent me the notice wasn't worth the expended energy.

"Let me check my schedule." I heard papers rustling, then, "I'm free for the next hour, if that suits you. The cost for a copy of the complete bylaws is three hundred dollars, and I can take a check or cash, but not a credit card. As for the form, you can make a photocopy, but your signature has to be original."

I know that jaw-dropping is a cliché, but when I realized my jaw had indeed dropped, I snapped my mouth shut. This also served to prevent me from blurting out anything I would regret.

For people in this community, three hundred dollars was a drop in the proverbial bucket. I mean, I spend more than that on a decent bottle of wine or dinner for two at Normandie. Our monthly HoA fee was more than that.

You'd think the fee would include a copy of the bylaws, but apparently not.

There wasn't a branch of our bank near our house, so I logged in to the bank's website, said a few words, and transferred out three hundred dollars in hundred-dollar bills. They appeared on my desk.

I yawned. The spell had taken enough energy out of me that I needed at least one more cup of coffee before I went to see Anastacia.

Gods and Goddesses, I hated this kind of unnecessary, over-layered bureaucracy.

THE BYLAWS WERE GATHERED in a black three-ring binder with a two-inch spine. The binder smelled every so faintly of mildew, and the pages inside had been photocopied multiple times. For three hundred dollars, I'd have expected something a little...classier. And a new printout. And a bottle of wine.

Pity it was too early to start drinking

Back in my home office, I flipped through the pages to find the relevant section. The numbers, though, ended before they reached the particular bylaw I was looking for. A note at the end of the section said that bylaws added since this edition could be found...

Morrigan's breath, you had to be kidding me.

Found *online*.

So while the bulk of the bylaws were still paper only, all of the additions and amendments were digital.

Not the form I needed, mind you. It existed only in the notebook, copied so many times it was faint and crooked.

Basically, it gave a space for me to explain why the infraction I'd been charged with wasn't really an infraction. (There was also a typo on it.)

I copied it one more time, but I didn't fill it out or sign it.

I went to law school, although I hadn't taken the bar either in New York or here. But one thing I knew was this: you don't sign a contract unless you understand it and agree with it.

I really wanted it to be time for a drink, but I sighed and got myself a lemon-infused soda water and went to work. Starting with page one of the damn bylaws.

THE PAGES WEREN'T NUMBERED PROPERLY, due to various inserts, so I had no idea how much I'd read when I was done. At least two hundred pages, which were now bristling with Post-It notes. Then I turned my attention to the additions and addendums and appendices online.

A few moments later, I realized I had to print those out, too, so I could mark them up.

The bylaws were a jumble of information that no longer applied, and conflicting rules and regulations, including new rules that contradicted old rules, and so forth. Instead of reviewing the bylaws when new laws were made, the new laws had simply been slapped on the end (or, for the past ten years or so, online).

And some of those new laws...

I texted the girls, and made plans for lunch the next day.

If we were going to get together to talk about this problem, we were going to do it well away from our houses and the potential for prying eyes.

BEFORE WE LEFT, we raised wards around our cars, and we each wore one of Shay's protective amulets, which were also designed to alert us if any other magic was used nearby.

We were probably being silly and overdramatic, but witches haven't survived as long as they have by letting their guard down.

This wasn't an inquisition, of course, but it felt like we were planning a skirmish and you don't go into war without armor, do you?

We'd picked a restaurant near the harbor, and took a table on the back patio, which was otherwise empty of patrons. Our heels clicked on the wooden floor as we made our way to our table, which was shaded by a big cloth umbrella. After taking our drink orders, the waiter left, leaving us with the sound of the breeze through the leaves of the plants providing privacy and the call of the gulls overhead. From the harbor came the twin scents of brine and diesel fuel.

We kept our conversation to lighter things—some Solstice fundraising news, some gossip—while we ate. After I finished my seared ahi salad and the waiter had whisked my plate away, I dropped the binder on the table with a thud.

The other three stared at it, astonished.

"How did we not know about this?" Shay asked.

"We never cared," Vanessa said with a sigh. "I know when we first moved in, it wasn't much of a problem. But Anastacia had just joined the board; she hadn't stepped up as president."

"Complaints started ramping up after that," Felisha said.

"How long has she been president?" I asked.

Vanessa pursed her crimson lips, frowning just enough to not wrinkle her forehead but still conveying her emotion. "About five years?"

"Closer to ten, I think," Felisha said.

"I remember her questioning me about having a home business," Shay said. "Yeah, eight or nine."

"She never gets voted off?" Maybe I don't understand how HoAs work.

Felisha shrugged. "Guess the rest of the board is happy not to have the responsibility."

"Like I said, we've never been to a meeting," Vanessa added.

"Well, we might just need to go to the next one," I said.

"It's the last one before Solstice, and I have some serious questions about their newest regulations."

I flipped open the book, paging through until I was close to the end where the most recent regulations were listed.

"For example, look at this," I said, pointing. "'Solstice rituals are prohibited from including interaction with the dead, as that is reserved for Samhain.' We were going to use our smaller ritual to help you gain closure from Vanessa's husband's death. It can't be a coincidence that this was voted in last month." It helped that the regulations were dated, because I hadn't had the chance to ask Anastacia for copies of meeting minutes. Those probably cost a kidney.

Not all the stupid rules related to witchcraft. California had water-rationing laws in place, but our lawns were required to be green (not to mention a specific height in inches) and our cars were required to be clean (even though they weren't allowed to be parked in our driveways for more than fifteen minutes at a time). The drain on magic to make these things happen could be exhausting—long-term spells were much harder on the body and psyche than one-off magics.

Other regulations had specific rules similar to the one about communicating with the dead at Solstice, such as when holiday decorations (for any holiday) could go up and when they had to be taken down. We were required to use cool white instead of warm white LEDs for outside decoration. (I hadn't realized there were two different kinds—my husband was going to have to go through our garage to find out which ones we had.)

Proscriptions about rituals, and what was appropriate for certain ones. Fire safety made sense, of course, but the height of one's altar? What color your gazing ball was?

I was sort of surprised there was nothing regarding whether it was okay to worship while skyclad, but many witches don't believe being naked is a requirement, so perhaps it had never come up.

Or maybe rules about nudity in one's own backyard would raise everyone's hackles, because if you wanted to tan all over...

Plus if they made a rule like that, how would they enforce it without being seen as voyeurs? (If they *did* make up some regulation about that, you'd better believe I'd be having sex with my husband by the pool on a regular basis.)

But I was getting distracted.

"Basically, it looks as though they've been ramping up on things for years," I said, "but the last year or so they've been firing off new rules left and right. I wonder why."

"Isn't it obvious?" Felisha said, turning her dark gaze on me. "It's you."

Shay gasped. "Of course."

Vanessa murmured an assent as well.

"*Me?* What did *I* do?"

"You moved here eight months ago," Felisha said. "Antastacia is threatened by you. It's not anything you did. It's how powerful you are."

My head felt light, as if I'd consumed many more mimosas than I had. This was ridiculous. "I'm not that powerful," I protested.

"You are," Shay said. Her silver and bead bracelets jangled as she reached out to put a soft, cool hand over mine. "You're the strongest witch in the community."

Vanessa leaned forward, and I felt the power behind her words rise before she even started speaking. "Magic is all about intention and focus, and those are two things you're very, very good at in any situation," she said.

"I'm—" I caught myself before I repeated myself, and changed it to a simple, "Thank you."

"Don't thank us," Shay said. "It's just the truth."

"But Anastacia isn't a hereditary witch," I protested. "We don't even have the same type of power. It's like eye of newt and toe of frog."

Shay snorted.

"Doesn't matter to people like her," Felisha said. "She might even be equating her power in the HoA with your power. Either way, I'm willing to bet my best athame that she sees you as some sort of threat."

"What's she trying to gain, then?" I asked. "A lot of these regulations don't target me specifically."

"True," Vanessa said. "Good question. All the more reason to go to the next meeting."

"Agreed," I said. "I'm not going to go in as an antagonist, but I'll definitely have my shields up."

THE FINAL HoA meeting of the year took place the following week. We had a week and a half until the big Solstice ritual and fundraiser, so we were already busy enough. As the day of the meeting grew closer, I found myself wanting to go less and less.

Too much work, I told myself. Plus I wanted to spend the evening with my husband. I wanted to order in and put our feet up and catch up on our Netflix shows, not freshen my makeup and go out.

Maybe we were overthinking things, assuming ulterior

motives when there were really none to be found. We could go next month, right?

The others could go without me, I decided, but when I texted them, I discovered they were all feeling tired, worn down, reluctant to go.

Sure, Solstice was coming up soon, but we had things well in hand. It was too much of a coincidence that we were *all* dragging our heels.

I called them up via SkyCall, the witches' version of Skype. (Any clear mirror will suffice.)

"It's a spell," I said. "I asked around last week, and I couldn't find anybody who goes to the meetings except for the board. They have to be putting up an avoidance ward or something."

Vanessa shook her head. "Why didn't I think of that?"

"None of us did," Felisha said. "So let's fight this spell. Shay?"

"Bring your amulets over tomorrow and we'll add extra protection to them, with an emphasis on creating a counterspell," Shay said immediately. She winked. "We'll do it inside to avoid Peeping Toms."

Or a watching witch...

THE FOUR OF us stood in a semicircle on the sidewalk, facing Anastacia's house. The doorway to the three-story Mediterranean-style house was brightly lit with wrought-iron sconces, and matching solar sconces lined the walkway.

We could feel the nudge of the spell surrounding the house, encouraging us to walk away, go find something else to do. It wasn't menacing or dangerous, just a pushback.

I hadn't felt it the day I'd picked up the HoA binder,

which was in my large, burgundy Prada tote. She must have either dropped the spell when she knew I was coming over, or set it up a few days before each meeting.

I squared my shoulders. "Let's do this," I said.

The others nodded and fell into line behind me. I hadn't intended to take the lead or take point on this mission, but I suppose it made sense. Anastacia seemed to have a problem with me, so I might as well be in charge of facing her.

When Anastacia opened the door, she blinked in surprise at the four of us standing there.

"Oh!" she said. "Oh...hello, dears. How can I help you?"

She was wearing a chic off-white pantsuit and her usual chunky gold jewelry. Her hair was the pale blond older women turn to when they're pretending they aren't really going gray, and perfectly coiffed. I smelled Nag Champa, the incense of witches around the world.

"We're here for the meeting," I said.

Her blue eyes narrowed, just slightly. I had no idea if she sensed the anti-spell wards on our amulets, but if she did, she didn't say or do anything. Pasting on a clearly fake smile, she stepped back and said, "Of course! Come in, dears."

The Mediterranean theme carried inside, unsurprisingly. Vaulted ceilings with exposed, dark wood beams made the place seem vast, especially with the floor covered with broad terra-cotta-hued tiles that made sounds louder.

The formal living area was off to the left and two wide steps down. A large, carved wooden pentagram hung over the stuccoed fireplace. The six other board members sat in a semicircle of coffee-brown leather sofas and overstuffed chairs. All had equally surprised looks on their faces, but stood to exchange air kisses with us.

Anastacia stood looking discomfited, until one of the

members—Adam, a retired professional baseball player/current entrepreneur—grabbed some padded straight chairs from around what looked like a gaming or tea table. There wasn't really room to put them between the other furniture, so we sat a little behind, able to see through the gaps.

As we'd suspected, nobody else from the community came to the meetings on any regular basis.

The plus side was, other than Anastacia's reaction, I didn't get the sense from the rest of the members that they were uncomfortable with us being here. My gut said they didn't know what Anastacia had been doing—or if they did, they weren't fully on board with it.

They did a brief energy ritual to seal a Circle around us, and Anastacia called the meeting to order. Most of the meeting was the usual business stuff: reviewing the minutes from last month, authorizing funds to drain and clean one of the ponds, someone's lawn not up to code, double toil and trouble, etc.

"One final vote tonight, and then we can wrap things up," Anastacia said. She hadn't looked at me or the girls since the meeting had started, her gaze skimming past us when she looked at the other board members. "As we discussed briefly last month, we'd like to make a change to the following regulation." She rattled off a number. I paged quickly through the binder but before I could find the relevant part, she went on. "The charity benefitting from the Winter Solstice fundraiser must be at least approved six months prior to the date of the ritual and fundraiser, effective immediately. All in favor?"

All four of us gasped. My hand shot up, and Anastacia was forced to acknowledge me. She kept her face composed and even sounded vaguely pleasant when she said, "Yes, dear?"

She probably thought she had the board in the palm of her hand.

"Aren't you supposed to open the floor for comments and questions before someone makes a motion and someone else seconds it and then you vote?"

I made it sound innocent, but here was the thing: I know *Robert's Rules of Order* better than I know some of our sacred texts. This *was* the hill I was willing to die on, metaphorically speaking.

"Well, yes, of course," she said, now looking annoyed. "But I think we know how we're all going to vote."

"I'm open to discussion," Adam said, looking at me. It was possible he was flirting with me. Well, I'd flirt back if it meant I'd win his vote, but I'd rather it didn't come to that.

Vanessa spoke up. "We announced the charity, Milo's Sanctuary, at Samhain as usual. That's been the procedure for years."

"Plus if you're going to change a rule, it shouldn't be retroactive," Felisha added. "The new regulation shouldn't take effect until the following year."

"If it even passes," Shay chimed in.

"What's the reason behind the proposed change?" I asked.

Anastacia said something about the board wanting more time to review the choice.

"Has the board ever rejected a suggested charity?" Felisha asked. "It hasn't in my memory. Or has the board had an issue with a charity after the fact?"

"I'd have to check the minutes," said Mary Anne, the board secretary. "But I think not."

"A lot can happen in six months," I said. "I can see

asking for a list of suggestions by the Summer Equinox, with any reservations or concerns returned to the committee by, say, Lammas. Then we can handle any coordination and have things locked in by Samhain."

"Why don't we table this until next month, so we have time to investigate and consider this new information," Adam suggested. "That way the change wouldn't be retroactive and affect this year, too."

"Is that a motion?" Anastacia asked. Adam nodded.

"Seconded," Mary Anne said.

The vote to table the discussion passed, with Anastacia grudgingly raising her hand when she saw the entire board disagreed with her. She was clearly furious, but holding herself together.

I was just grateful that she couldn't literally shoot daggers from her eyes.

Anastacia tried to end the meeting, but I raised my hand again and said I had a question. She formally recognized me (I didn't even get a "dear"). I said I'd brought my form to protest the write-up of having an unsanctioned ritual of more than four people, since we hadn't been having a ritual, but a planning meeting.

"We enforce that?" one of the board members said with surprise, but I didn't catch who.

Anastacia ignored that question and tersely asked me what mine was. I asked how the board had received the information when my backyard wasn't visible from the street or by my neighbors.

Anastacia sputtered and demurred, finally citing an anonymous tip. I knew, from reading the entire poorly photocopied binder, that anonymous tips were acceptable (to keep the peace, so one neighbor doesn't know which neighbor tattled on them). I could have argued that that anonymous person had broken the law—as in, state or federal law—but I let it go because Anastacia was already accepting my form and canceling my fine.

We'd won a couple of battles, but not the war. And I still wasn't even sure what the war was about.

~

ANASTACIA KEPT quiet in the days leading up to the Solstice. At least, she didn't contact the four of us. We weren't sure whether to be relieved or concerned.

She might have something planned during the ritual or fundraiser, and we were determined that she wasn't going to ruin the holiday.

~

SOLSTICE EVE HELD a hint of welcomed crispness, with a clear sky sparkling with stars. (The community walls had an ongoing spell built in that reduced light pollution from the surrounding cities.) Although I'd been enjoying the escape from winter, the closer the holiday came, the more I missed snow, or at least December weather. Winter Solstice in New York City was (pardon the pun) magical in the glittering snow.

One of the other residents in the community owned a high-end party planning firm, which had been hired for years to handle the decorations. I had no reference to what previous years had been like, but this year the community hall was stunning.

The main room, where the ritual would be performed, had been turned into a winter forest wonderland, a sacred grove for sacred rituals. The trees, which covered the walls and grew over the edges of the ceiling, looked and felt real, the bark rough, the branches of the oak and ash stark, the yews and hollies lush green and dotted with red berries.

Above, the ceiling showed the midnight-blue of twilight, with a crescent moon and stars. The room smelled of loam and pine, and I would have sworn the leaves were rustling.

In the center of the room, a rough-hewn stone altar carved with spirals, and on the altar, the tools of our trade: chalice and athame, wand and bundle of dried sage and lavender.

Despite the insistence that I was the most powerful witch in the community, it had never been in the plan to have me officiate the Solstice ritual. I was too new to the area. And I was perfectly fine with that.

The rest of the community entered the room, forming concentric circles. The thirteen of us followed, carrying unlit, fat white pillar candles, and the circles parted to allow us into the center. I felt odd being in the core thirteen, but everyone else had welcomed me warmly. We walked around the altar three times, then twelve of us formed a final circle with Felisha, serving as High Priestess for the evening, in the center next to the altar.

We set the candles in a ring around the altar, and straightened.

We were in the sacred space that we all had created. Magic hummed as each woman drew power from the earth and sky. For me, it was like a tingling just under my skin, and a sense of pure joy.

This was the community-wide ritual, whereas later, Vanessa, Shay, Felisha, and I would have a private one, to work on our personal issues—HoA rules or not.

Given what we'd been dealing with in the past few

weeks, we'd made minor modifications to this ritual. Winter Solstice was the longest night of the year, the shortest day. It was a celebration of the coming longer days, the Wheel turning and bringing us spring, and new growth, and also a reflection of the past year and a farewell to the seasonal darkness. It was a time of letting go of something negative, and letting in something positive—things individual to each person.

We as witches were also guardians of the earth. We were responsible to nature, to energy, to balance.

Given not only the recent events but what had been going on in the world at large, we'd realized we needed to bring everyone together and call up energy for a greater purpose.

Felisha, with her melodious voice, guided us through the opening stages of the ritual: the calling of the guardians of the four directions; dipping the blade into the chalice to honor the balance of feminine and masculine, Goddess and God; honoring the Holly King who dies this night, and welcoming the Oak King who will usher us into summer.

"Winter Solstice," Felisha said. "The Wheel turns. Darkness into light. In our homes, and around the world, witches will banish something negative, something holding them back, and embrace something positive to bring into the growing light and embody in the coming year."

"So mote it be," the rest of us intoned.

"Here, though, we gather together for greater purposes. We are the guardians of the Earth, our Mother. We are the protectors of her flame, and we champion her when she is in need."

"So mote it be."

"To do that, we care for each and every person. We are

all connected. We are all imperfect, but we are all worthy. Guarding the Earth, our Mother, starts here, with each other. Here, in this community, and the country, and across the world."

"So mote it be."

Everyone in the room was raising energy. Through our clasped hands and through our hearts, we sent it deosil, clockwise, left hand to right. In the end, we'd release it out into the world, sending it where it needed to go, to people in crisis, to land in crisis.

When Felisha said *community*, however, the four of us nudged some extra energy at Anastacia, trying to underscore the point.

We hoped it would weaken her hold on the community —more by giving everyone strength to resist the compulsions she brewed—but also remind her that community was more important than the individual. We didn't attack, except with love and compassion.

Anastacia nudged back.

I glanced around the inner circle. Nobody else seemed to have noticed. The nudge had been for me personally.

I hadn't wanted to do this alone. I'd really, really hoped Anastacia would get the message, take the hint, see that she was focusing in the wrong direction.

But the others had been right: for some reason, I was on her personal shit list.

The Circle we'd raised was supposed to be a safe place, a space of love and trust. For that reason, none of us were wearing our amulets; they would have been counter to the energy here.

We never thought Anastacia would act out here, during the ritual.

I reached inside for a protection spell, a way to raise

shields around myself that wouldn't block the flow of the energy swirling in the room but that would give me a barrier against Anastacia, but I was too late.

The world tilted, sideways and back again, and I was no longer in the room.

I was no longer in my *body*.

Well, that was a little disconcerting.

The astral plane was everything and nothing, black and white and every color and yet no color at all. Because I had no body, I didn't have the five normal bodily senses. Everything was *feeling*, an inner sense rather than an outer one.

Hereditary witches know the astral plane instinctively. I had no idea where or how Anastacia had learned to access it.

Why? I asked. *What did I ever do to you?*

No response.

I'm not your enemy, I added. *None of us are. Is there something you need—?*

Something slammed into me, or, rather, into my noncorporeal consciousness. Then a jerk, as if she was trying to pull something out of me.

Energy. Power.

She wanted it, I had it.

Oh, she wanted to play this game, did she?

She had more power than she should have, certainly, but she was no match for me. I responded in kind, reaching out with tendril non-fingers and delving into the part of her that was in the astral plane.

I latched on to her core, the place where power was stored. And I pulled.

She shrieked without sound and yet I somehow heard it. She struggled against me, fought to stop me from dragging the power out of her, hand over hand like pulling up an anchor, but she didn't have the knowledge or the skill.

I pulled her power to me, wrapped it into a ball that in my mind's eye glowed gold and silver both, and kept packing it tighter and smaller until I could "carry" it with me.

I didn't take everything—the last thing I wanted to do was cause her harm, either astrally or physically. But I took enough that apparently she could no longer hold us here.

I came back to my body with a jolt, stumbling with one foot forward before pulling myself together (literally). Felisha shot me a concerned look, and I raised my chin in a nod to let her know I was okay.

I couldn't see Anastacia—she'd been somewhere in the crowd behind me. The ritual was continuing, and I had to focus on it.

Felisha urged us to increase the flow of energy through our bound hands, faster and faster until it began spiraling up. As one, we released our grips and raised our hands up, firing the magic up into the world, to land where it was most needed.

When we did that, I sent Anastacia's power along with my own and everyone else's, choosing to spread it through our community or beyond.

After all, that was the point of having magic.

ANASTACIA HAD SCURRIED out the door as soon as the Circle was lowered. We focused on the refreshments and the fundraiser, which went very well indeed.

The next day, she was gone. Her house was empty, and before long a For Sale sign appeared on the yellowing lawn.

Slowly, over the next month or two, facts and information trickled in, allowing us to piece together the overall picture.

It turned out Anastacia had developed a bit of a gambling problem after her husband died. She'd been skimming off the HoA dues as well as the more frequent fines for new violations. The other board members hadn't even known about some of the violations and fines she'd levied, meaning those funds had gone directly into her pocket.

On top of that, she'd been getting off on the power of being in control, of policing the community. As in, it had been allowing her to increase her magical abilities to the level of a hereditary witch. She'd always felt left out, lesser, and when her husband died, that had turned into something of an obsession. Apparently she thought the increased power would help her with the aforementioned gambling.

In our private ritual on Winter Solstice night, Vanessa found closure with her dead ex-husband, Shay found ways to control her menopausal energy surges, and Felisha came to Goddess about her kids having grown up and moved away.

Me? I'd already solved my own problem. I needed a project.

And the HoA needed an interim president to clean up the mess Anastacia had made.

All that, and I didn't even break a nail.

GIVING TO THE NIGHT

Maggie accepted the cup of tea from the waiter and forced a smile. It wouldn't be fair to be rude to him just because she wasn't feeling friendly. "Thank you," she said. "Happy holidays."

The ruse apparently didn't work, because instead of walking away, he said, "You don't sound like they're very happy."

She considered the plain white teacup before her, cradling her hands around it for warmth. "I'm sorry. It's just...well, this was probably the wrong time of year to tell my parents that I...don't share their religious beliefs."

"And you had a row," the waiter concluded. "Finally came out of the broom closet, eh?"

Startled, Maggie finally looked up at him, unable to suppress a sudden laugh. "I've never heard it called that before. But how did you—?"

He nodded at her necklace, and she realized how he'd figured out she was pagan. Here in Glastonbury, it didn't bother her to wear the pentagram openly, something she wasn't used to. But there were far stranger things to be seen in this New Age mecca in the southwest of England.

The waiter, now that she looked at him properly, proved to be quite attractive, with longish brown hair, blue eyes, and a friendly smile that didn't fade as he dropped into the chair opposite hers. The tea shop wasn't crowded; the lunch rush had left and the tea-time regulars hadn't arrived.

"So did you fly all the way here to get away from them?" he asked.

Maggie opened her mouth to ask how he'd known she was American, then remembered her accent (or lack of it. For some reason, British people thought Americans had the accent, not the other way around.).

"Not exactly," she said. It was so nice to have someone talk to that she didn't feel strange telling him the story. "I'm studying over here, doing graduate work. I was going to go home for the holidays, but after arguing with my parents, I didn't see the point."

She didn't know how to explain to them how she felt. How could she describe the energy that spiraled up in her and made her feel a part of everything? How could she explain the utter rightness of a dual God and Goddess? How could she demonstrate that the love and respect she felt for the Earth went beyond a simple ecological whim? They just wouldn't understand.

"Do you have a place to stay?" the waiter asked.

She smiled. The holiday spirit of giving was alive and well here. "Yes, thank you. I've rented a self-catering cottage for the month." The smile turned rueful. "It's just a little bare because I didn't bring much with me when I came over to study, and most of that I left in my dorm room. It's just me and my books and my laptop right now."

The cafe door opened, letting in a gust of chill air, the smell of rain, and a huddle of teenage goths. Maggie's waiter stood.

"Back to work," he said. "Enjoy your tea, witchy babe."

MAGGIE RETURNED to the tea shop the next day, in large part because she was a terrible cook but, she knew, also in part because she hoped to meet the friendly waiter again. To her dismay, he'd been replaced by a blond girl with bright blue eyeliner and studs in her nose and right eyebrow (and who knew where else). Maggie spent the next two days on buses exploring the Uffington White Horse, the Long Man of Wilmington, and the Cerne Abbas Giant— figures cut into the chalk hillsides in Dorset and Wiltshire —and Stonehenge and the Avebury stone circles. She returned more grounded and centered (and laden with even more books on British pagan traditions), but still depressed about her inability to get through to her parents.

So she was somewhat surprised when she returned and had her tea delivered by the charming waiter who not only remembered her, but handed her a plastic carrier bag, saying,

"I was hoping you'd come back, witchy babe. I thought these might brighten up your flat."

The bag revealed a tangle of metal and rainbow color. She gently tipped the contents out onto the Formica tabletop and sorted it.

It turned out to be a variety of silver wire ornaments shaped like pentacles and crescent moons and fiery suns and spirals, with vibrant glass beads interwoven throughout. The jewel tones glittered in the fluorescent light of the cafe as she held one up.

"They're beautiful!" Maggie cried.

The waiter suddenly seemed a little shy. "They're Yule ornaments to hang on your tree. You do have a tree in that bare little flat of yours, don't you?"

She bit her lip. "Well, no.... I could hang them around the room, though. They'll look wonderful in the windows." She picked up another and watched it sparkle in the light. "These really are gorgeous. Where did you get them?"

He shoved his hands in his pockets, a charming display of sudden bashfulness. "I made them."

Maggie's face must have shown her astonishment, because he added, "I'm an artist. I've been selling wire sculptures in shops in town for awhile now. I'm hoping to get a commission on a bigger piece soon—the town council is putting up a sculpture up next year and one of the designs they're considering is mine."

"I'm very impressed," Maggie said. She felt a little teary-eyed at his generosity—she didn't even know his name! But before she could ask, they were again interrupted by a flurry of customers, enough that she felt she had to vacate her table to allow enough space for them. She walked by the tea shop later in the afternoon, but didn't see him inside.

THE NEXT DAY she went back, this time with a thank-you card and the goal of at least learning his name. Her disappointment at seeing the blond girl again turned to amazement when the young woman cheerfully greeted her, vanished into the kitchen, and returned with a small potted evergreen that she deposited in front of Maggie.

"Ian said you didn't have a Yule tree," she said by way of explanation. When Maggie tried to demur, she added, "My dad has a nursery, so I got it cheap. If you can't take it back to university with you, we're planting a sacred grove in the spring and we'll add it there if you like."

Well. Maggie hugged her new tree as she leaned into the chill evening wind. At least now she knew his name.

It continued like that over the next few days: either Ian or one of his friends—who seemed to consider Maggie a friend by default—arrived with a small offering for the holidays. There were crystals and shells and pinecones and dried flowers ("For your altar, dear," the middle-aged woman said), a corn dolly, a hand-thrown bowl, a purple silk scarf painted with the Goddess and the God. None of the people would take "no" for an answer, and when she protested to Ian, he smiled and said there was nothing he could do about it. And then he would suggest they take a walk.

It didn't feel wrong when he gently took her hand one morning as they wandered through Glastonbury, ducking into different shops each time it started to spit rain. Ian was familiar with all the shops, of course, and Maggie appreciated his patience as she examined everything inside, oohed and ahhed, and asked a million questions.

"I've read a few books, but mainly I just know that it feels right," she said of paganism. "Sometimes I'm overwhelmed by how much there is to learn."

He turned to her. "What's important," he said, "is how

you feel here—" and he placed a hand on her jacket just above her breast "—and here—" and his palm rested on her stomach. He tapped her on the temple. "What you think here isn't inconsequential, but it's not the most important thing."

She felt a tingle at each place where he touched her. Not magic, she knew, but something much more personal.

On another day, they climbed Glastonbury Tor, the alleged Isle of Avalon, to watch the sun set. Someone had strewn fresh pine boughs in the tower, and they breathed in the sharp holiday scent. Ian had a heavy grey cloak and he flung it over both of them against the chill. It felt so right to lean against him, feeling the beat of his heart beneath his woolly cream cable-knit sweater, and talk quietly of magic and symbols and history as the clouds in the west bloomed orange and rose and carmine.

It was there, under the flowering sunset, that they first kissed.

Maggie felt the earth tilt beneath her, and yet she had no fear, because she knew without knowing how that she was firmly connected to the ground. The first sprinkling of stars in the sky spun above them like a spiral, no beginning and no ending.

The world seemed infinite in space and possibility, and yet, at the same time, it shrank to encompass her and Ian and their embrace.

THE EVE of the Solstice broke the pattern of the week's rainy weather, and diamond stars glittered in the velvet sky, joined by a thin sickle moon. With the clear weather came the inevitable bite of cold, so Maggie put on her warmest sweater, an oversized red monstrosity, and shoved a matching cap on her head. Despite the cold, she went outside to wait for Ian to arrive to take her to the Solstice celebration. It gave her time to think about what he'd said.

"This is primarily a party—a celebration," Ian had explained. "However, in the past few years we've starting doing a small…I'm not even sure if 'ritual' is the right word. It's more like a meditation. You're not expected to join in so don't feel pressured to participate if you don't want to. I just want to let you know what to expect."

"Go on," Maggie said, intrigued.

"We always build a bonfire in the backyard—"

"Oh, that's fine," Maggie said dryly. "I'm not afraid of fire."

Ian laughed. Maggie liked the unselfconscious way he let loose his amusement.

"That's a start, then," he said. "Anyway, as you know, the Solstice is the longest night of the year. So, we each pick something to give up to the night—something negative. If you want, you can decide what to put in its place, although for me that doesn't usually come until later in the year. It's a sense of opening a space up for something positive to enter."

What did she want to give up to the night? Maggie wondered again as she waited in the crisp midwinter night. What did she want to unburden herself of? She shoved her hands deep into the pockets of her jeans and stared up at the glittering stars, and delved within herself. It wasn't an easy question. It seemed far safer to flinch away from negative thoughts, negative emotions. But part of what religion was for her was personal growth and betterment. If she wasn't willing to face the negatives within herself, and if she wasn't brave enough to let them go, then she couldn't open herself up to something more beneficial.

Ian's battered Mini rolled up and he jumped out before she could reach for the door handle. "Well, hello there," he said, sounding pleased. He took her cold hands, leaned in, and softly kissed her. Each time they kissed, it sent a shock-wave through her. *Ground*, she told herself firmly. It would do no good to be crackling with extraneous energy—at least, not yet.

Anne, the blond with the piercings, was hosting the party at her house outside of Glastonbury. Ian drove them through narrow winding lanes bordered by high hedgerows, pulling over in wider areas to let other cars squeeze past, their headlights flashing their thanks.

Maggie was surprised by how many people she knew at the gathering: It seems all of Ian's friends who'd "adopted" her over the past two weeks were there. She gladly accepted a pint of Guinness and before she knew it, was pulled in to a conversation about Green Man images and his counterpart, the sheela-na-gig. Ian stayed at her side, often with a hand resting lightly on her waist.

She liked his touch, and the smell of whatever soap he used, and the easy but intimate way he chatted with his friends. He cared about these people.

When the pencils and slips of paper were passed out, she still hadn't decided what to give up to the night, but she'd long since resolved to participate in the ritual. She smiled and nodded at Ian's questioning glance, and he smiled back, obviously relieved that she wasn't uncomfortable. They followed everyone outside to the cleared, rock-ringed space where a bonfire cheerfully pushed back the confines of the longest, darkest night.

After a moment's stillness so everyone could focus in his or her own way, people began scribbling on their papers. Maggie glanced at Ian. He was staring intently into the fire, brow furrowed slightly. She found a little surprised. He'd done this ritual before—shouldn't it be easy for him by now? Hadn't he given up enough negative things already? Goodness, he should be perfect by now! She smiled at her own silliness, at the very presumption that he couldn't continue to better himself.

And with that thought, she realized what she needed to do.

Maggie spread out the scrap of paper on her knee, wrote a single word, and firmly folded the paper several times. She stepped toward the fire and tossed the paper in, watching it catch alight and disappear into the flames. As it turned to ashes and smoke that drifted away, she willed, so would the negative....

THEY STAYED at the party awhile longer, laughing and talking and drinking mulled cider, until most folks started drifting off or preparing to bed down in Anne's living room. The drive home was in companionable silence; Maggie's hand rested lightly on Ian's knee and when he wasn't shifting, he covered her hand with his own.

They stopped in front of her flat, but neither made a move to exit the car.

"Thank you," Maggie said finally. "I had a wonderful time tonight. Goodness, that sounds so trite!" she added with a laugh. "I mean it, though. Your friends have all been so kind to me, and you..."

He squeezed her hand. "I'm glad," he said finally. His

voice seemed to come from far away, as if he hadn't been sure he could speak.

"What did you give to the night?" Maggie blurted. She flushed. "I'm sorry—that's probably the pagan equivalent of asking a woman her age."

He stared ahead, and she watched his profile: the strong line of his cheekbone highlighted by the streetlight, the unfocus of his eyes.

"That's okay," he said finally. His smile filled her with a rush of relief. "I don't mind telling you. I gave up fear. I've lived here all my life, I've known these people all my life, and recently I've started realizing that to have what I want, I might have to leave."

A curious warm feeling spread through Maggie's chest. But before she could ask another question, Ian broached his.

"And what, my witchy babe, did you give to the night— but tell me only if you want to."

Maggie turned her hand so that their fingers laced together. "It took me awhile to find the right word, and what I used may not be exact, but I know what I was trying to say, what I was feeling."

"That's the important thing," he murmured.

"Presumption," she said.

"What?"

"Presumption." Maggie took a deep breath. "Looking at something and thinking it was the only way. I was presuming that paganism was simple, and I realized that I couldn't truly learn more unless I accepted how much more there was. I assumed my parents wouldn't understand, and barely gave them the chance to listen to what I was saying before cut them off. They were upset, yes, but I didn't give them the benefit of a real conversation." She took another long breath. Fear was a good thing to give up, too. She had to take the chance that she'd interpreted his words correctly. "And I presumed that when my scholarship to study here ends in June, I'd go home."

"So what are you going to do, witchy babe?" Ian's breath warmed her cheek; he was leaning quite close to her. She could smell the bonfire smoke in his hair. Maggie turned her head to face him.

"Well," she said, "it's still early in the U.S., so I'm going to call my parents. Then, when I get back to the university, I'm going to see if there's a way to extend my studies here, or what other possibilities there might be.

"As for everything else..." and she leaned so close that her lips brushed his "...I'll just have to not presume, and see where it takes me."

Maggie tried very hard not to presume anything from their ensuing kiss.

WHO WE'LL BECOME
A VALDEMAR STORY

We sing to bring light to the darkness
We sing to welcome the sun
We sing of family and loved ones
We sing of a new year begun...

The traditional Midwinter song filled the great hall of Traynemarch Reach's manor, the children's voices imperfect but heartfelt, the melody soaring up to the high, dark rafters and swirling around the listeners. It mingled with the fire blazing in the stone hearth draped with ivy and holly and fragrant pine boughs.

The longest night, the shortest day, and the Midwinter Feast that brought family and friends together.

Syrriah had missed the last two years' celebration at Traynemarch Reach, her old home. This homecoming was bittersweet. The familiar song brought sparkling tears to her eyes.

Three years ago, she had been the Lady of Traynemarch Reach, and she and her husband were preparing to pass their roles on to Syrriah's sister and brother-in-law. A wintery river and a collapsed bridge in need of repair had changed everything. Of course Syrriah's husband had helped the villagers. The resulting chill he suffered grew worse—and then deadly.

Everything changed six months later, when the jangle of bells announced the arrival of a Companion.

Not a Companion ridden by one of Syrriah's four children, who had all already been Chosen.

A Companion for Syrriah.

This was the first time she'd been back home since that bewildering but ultimately rewarding day. Not a day went by when Syrriah wasn't astounded by the relationship she had with Cefylla.

Right now, despite the warmth of the fire in the hearth, the beautiful singing (which included her two youngest, Benlan and Natalli), and her family around her, Syrriah half-wished she were in the barn with Cefylla.

She heard a snort in her mind. *:Hardly,:* Cefylla said. *:It's a nice sentiment, but I rather think you'll enjoy your feast over my warm mash.:*

Syrriah bit back a laugh. *:There is that,:* she admitted. The long, white-cloth-covered table was laden with deep blue ceramic dishes and pitchers. The traditional foods: tender roast mutton and crispy-skinned duck, carrots and parsnips in a creamy dill sauce, small seed cakes decorated with suns made out of dried flower petals. Sweet summer wine, vinted especially for this feast. Between everything, dark blue candles representing the midwinter night sky, each flame a call to the rising sun at dawn.

She should have felt at home; after all, she'd been the Lady here for more than twenty years. But in the relatively short time she'd been away, Collegium, Cefylla, the Heralds...they'd become her life.

Plus, Riann, her sister (who Syrriah had named her oldest daughter for), well, she did things different. When Riann and her husband had stepped up to run the manor and holdings, Syrriah had offered her advice and assistance, but only if they asked. She respected and trusted them both.

And, certainly, the changes were not of any great import. If Riann preferred everyone wait until after the feast to open the cloth-wrapped gifts that sat above each dinner plate, that was her choice, even if it went against tradition and made the younger children fidget. (Riann's youngest kept reaching out and touching the fabric wrapping with a forefinger. Each time, his older sister nudged him, and he shoved the finger in his mouth. The food on his plate was largely untouched.)

The curtains covering the tall, stone-framed windows were different; Riann's preferred greens and blues to Syrriah's reds and golds. Syrriah would probably have a bruise on her left hip before she left, because the furniture in the main hall had been rearranged, and she could never remember to skirt that one chair.

Indeed, the new arrangement gave fresh life to the room, and Syrriah hadn't thought about colors since she went to Collegium—other than the colors the various trainees and Heralds wore. She was glad Riann and her husband had made Traynemarch Reach their own. And she'd heard nothing but good things about their stewardship of the holdings.

It just all took some getting used to, this familiar-but-not.

Waking up this morning had been strange as well. At Collegium, there was always the chatter of student voices in the halls in the morning, or outside her window as

Heralds and trainees returned from spending time with their Companions at the stable. Here, she could hear the crackle and snap of the icicles hanging from the eaves just outside. Plus, the room may have looked like Traynemarch Reach, but it wasn't the one she'd spent more than twenty years waking up in.

Her clothing was yet another matter.

She'd looked forward to wearing her old gowns, which she'd left behind, rather than her trainee gray tunic and loose pants and boots. She'd missed choosing what to wear each day.

Her gowns, however, no longer fitted her the same. She'd always been an active woman, but her training at Collegium, including a newfound affinity for archery, had reshaped her. Her gowns were looser in some places, but tighter than others, such as her shoulders and arms. She had to be careful not to raise her arms too high, or she might tear out a seam.

She felt constricted by that, and the heavy skirts, and was already longing for the simple comfort of her trainee grays.

She might have been able to brush off all of that if it hadn't been for one final thing:

She felt completely useless.

Oh, she'd struggled with that before being Chosen, but being Chosen had given her a new purpose—and that new life. Here, she was even more strongly reminded that she had no function at Traynemarch Reach.

"You're looking rather serious for a celebration," Riann, next to her, said with a gentle nudge of her elbow. Her voice was light, but Syrriah saw the concern in her blue eyes.

Syrriah's Gift of Empathy had broken free during her training at Collegium, and she wouldn't have been surprised to discover such a talent could run in a family to a lesser degree. Riann had always been kind and caring, as well as organized and intelligent, which was why Syrriah and Brant had chosen her to take over the manor.

Syrriah felt guilty for worrying Riann. As hostess, her sister had far more important things to worry about.

As the final notes of the song faded, she smiled, and squeezed Riann's hand.

"I'm fine," she said, and it wasn't entirely a lie. She was glad to be with her family, no matter how unsettling the changes were.

Or how useless she felt.

:You're quite useful,: Cefylla gravely informed her. *:In fact, if you're through eating, I could use a good brushing.:*

~

> We honor those who have passed on
> We honor the year now gone by
> We banish the darkness with kindness
> We rejoice when new dawn greets the sky...

THE NEXT DAY, the sun indeed did rise, with the day bright and clear, giving a sense of warmth even in the chill of the season. An auspicious start to the Midwinter Festival.

Syrriah's old riding gear proved more comfortable than her gowns, and her mood lightened as she rode on Cefylla alongside Riann and her husband, the rest of the household following behind along with a pack-horse laden with gifts. The chill in the air, the laughter and banter rising on visible, mist-like breath, the joy of the season. Hooves crunching on packed snow. Sweet smoke from chimneys. The glitter of the river in the distance; the fallow fields slumbering in preparation for spring planting.

As they rode through the village, Syrriah noticed what houses had new decorations, and the ones that had added a room or a new fence. Lives had continued, just as hers had.

They were joined by other riders, as well as families walking as they headed out the other side of the village. Eventually they came to the crossroads where the monthly market was held, drawing merchants from several nearby towns and villages.

The Midwinter Fair market, however, was a special event indeed.

People wore new clothing they'd been gifted, coats and hats and scarves. Children ran about, shrieking and laughing. The fair was a time to celebrate children, too, so shopkeepers had sweets or small toys to hand out.

In the center of the marketplace was a white-painted gazebo from which announcements were made and news was shared. Today, it was draped with pine boughs and silver-and-blue ribbons, and a small group of musicians with lute and drum and shawm performed traditional songs. Syrriah put coins in the basket they'd set out, and the lute player nodded and winked his thanks.

They left Cefylla and the horses at the public stable, and Lord and Lady Trayne, and their children, began the annual procession around the market, handing out small gifts and tokens. At first Syrriah accompanied them, but eventually she fell back, spending more time perusing the market wares.

At Collegium, she lived in a small room and her necessities were provided for: clothing, food, and so forth. She had little space for personal items, and she had brought things from home that were special to her, such a portrait of Brant, with a lock of each of her children's hair tucked under the glass.

She was busy enough at Collegium with her studies and training that leisurely shopping had also become a thing of the past. Now, she indulged in fingering some fine linen, a dark red chevron pattern shot through with gold. She sniffed the flowery perfumes and soaps, the jars of teas. She admired sheep fleeces and tanned leather and furs. Cheeses, wine, flour, and hops.

She knew many of the merchants, although there were always some who came and went. Some curtsied or bowed —even though she no longer ran Traynemarch Reach, there was still memory, and respect, and she was delighted to greet them all and learn how they had fared since her departure.

Eventually she came to the stall of one of her favorite artisans, a man everyone called Carver because of his incredible woodworking skills.

She breathed in the sweet smell of wood shavings, undercut with the cider he had in a pot on the small stove at the back of the stall. Heat from the stove took an edge off the day's chill.

By the front of the stall sat a basket filled with gifts for the children who came by, obviously made from pieces left over from other projects. Rings for fat baby fingers to grasp, dolls, blunt swords, blocks with letters on them.

She was greeted, not by Carver, but by his son, Eron.

The hair at Eron's brow had receded since the last time she'd seen him, but then, her own hair had new strands of silver shot through it. He was just as tall, just as wiry, with the same long-fingered, capable hands cross-hatched with pale scars from his work.

Both he and his sister, Vaice, were skilled woodworkers

in their own right. Some said even more talented—including Carver himself.

"Lady Trayne," he greeted her, his voice hearty and his brown eyes smiling. Then, with a small shake of his head: "I'm sorry—*Herald*. How are you?"

"I'm well, Eron. But please, I'm not a Herald yet. You can call me Herald-trainee, but here, now, I'd prefer Syrriah."

"'Tis strange to call you that, I confess, after all the years of you and your lord in the manor."

"My title may be different, but I've not changed," she said.

"Ah, but haven't we all?" he said, echoing her thoughts.

He offered her a cup of cider, which she gratefully accepted. Made from her favorite local apples, it was tart, warm, and laced with cinnamon and cloves.

Every piece Carver created was unique, a fact in which he took great pride. (Unless, of course, he made a set; then each part was indistinguishable from the next.) Every piece was solidly crafted, too. The cradle she had purchased almost twenty years ago had served her four babies well, before she had passed it on to Riann.

His skill was known throughout Valdemar, even though he could make only a certain number of large pieces each year.

She asked Eron about his father, and learned that Carver had recently passed the business on to Eron and Vaice. He was still carving small things, but didn't have the energy for larger pieces anymore.

Eron showed her the headboard he was carving for a wedding, and Vaice's latest project, a set of anniversary cups, the names of the couple's children spiraling along the bowl of each. The work on both was exquisite.

But underlying his words, masked by his smile, was a thread of unhappiness. Something troubled him. Syrriah tamped down on her Gift, not wanting to intrude. She was not the lady of the manor; she was not quite a friend. If it was something he wished her to know about, he would tell her.

She was just about to leave when Vaice ducked under the awning to the merchant stall.

Vaice was as tall as her brother and father, with the same wiry strength. Her light brown hair was plaited, the braids wrapped around her head to keep it out of the way while she worked.

They both must be nearing thirty now, Syrriah realized, no longer children at all, even though it was easy to still think of them that way.

As soon as Vaice entered, Eron's sense of being troubled flared.

"I was hoping to speak with you, actually," Vaice said to Syrriah after sketching a brief curtsy. "I was wondering when you planned to return to Haven."

"In a little more than a weeks' time," Syrriah said. "It will depend on the weather; I'll leave earlier if necessary."

Vaice bit her lip, clearly avoiding looking at her brother. "Would you...would you and your Companion be willing to let me ride with you? If I wouldn't slow you down, I mean."

"Surely you can wait until spring..." Eron said.

"I'm not changing my mind, so waiting won't make a difference," Vaice said.

Syrriah was a mother of four. She didn't need Empathy to hear the stubbornness in Vaice's voice, and see it in her squared shoulders and the jut of her jaw.

"Maybe this is something you can help us with," Eron

said, turning to Syrriah. "Give us your advice, based on your training."

Syrriah's training wasn't complete, but before she could point that out, Vaice said, "I'd be interested in hearing what you have to say. Especially if it means convincing my brother it makes no sense to be stuck in the past."

"We've been given a legacy," Eron said. "It's our job to uphold it—not destroy it."

It was clear they'd been having this argument for some time. They barely even seemed to hear each other's words.

The job of a Herald included diplomacy and negotiating skills. Syrriah wasn't a Herald yet, but as lady of the manor, she'd needed similar abilities.

Besides, this was a family dispute, not a situation in service to the Monarch.

She could pull Riann away from the Midwinter Fair—it was an issue that could very much affect the Major holdings, as the business brought wealth and commerce to Traynemarch Reach—or she could see if she could help.

"I'm willing to listen, and give my opinion," she said. "But not as a Herald; I'm still a trainee. As...an unbiased ear."

Vaice motioned her to a set of chairs in the corner. They were serviceable, solid, with clean lines. The grain of the wood gleamed with polish, and felt incredibly smooth. There wouldn't be a splinter to be found. They had a quiet beauty, and what Syrriah thought of as the Carver quality... although they bore none of the intricate carving she'd expected.

A moment later, she learned why.

Vaice went first. "I have been studying economics and business," she said. "My father made a good living for our family with his work, but now there are two of us, with two families. When Eron and I began helping Father, our output increased, but it has decreased, obviously, since he retired."

"We could bring in an apprentice," Eron said.

"Apprentices still need to be housed, and clothed, and fed," she countered. "And there's no guarantee they'd ever get to the skill level needed, or that they wouldn't leave to start their own business."

"You make good points," Syrriah said. "I'm guessing you have a solution?"

Vaice held out her hand. "You're sitting on them," she said. "We can make simpler items much faster—and we can hire people to help with the basic work. Set up work stations, even. So, for example, one person is turning spindles, another person is doing something else. We would make sure the quality was just as high as it is now, but be able to produce more. Plus, it would widen our customer base. So many people can't afford what we make, and these items would be priced cheaper."

Syrriah was knowledgeable enough to have helped with the books at Traynemarch Reach, but this was something she'd never considered. It made a great deal of sense.

"Eron?" she said.

He leaned back in his seat, arms across his chest, even as his body language betrayed that he didn't want to be sitting on this particular chair.

"Our business is known for the individual pieces my father, and then we, have crafted. He created a legacy from nothing, a heritage that we can't turn our backs on. It would devastate him."

He sighed. "But Vaice is right about the money, and I don't have an easy solution. We can look for a different supplier for lumber, but we'd have to be certain the quality wouldn't change. I don't want to charge more for what we make, but..."

Vaice nodded. "We probably could command more, but I don't think the higher prices would cover the fewer orders."

"You both agree that quality is paramount," Syrriah said.

They both nodded then.

She ran her hand along the silken-smooth arm of her chair. Could the solution be as easy as it seemed?

"It's true," she said, "that your father's business has always been known for the unique pieces he made, the gorgeously intricate carving and design. But I think that the other component was, as you both agree, quality."

She considered her next words. "Beauty can be found in many forms," she said. "In the intricate work of that head-board or those goblets, but also in the lines and the flow of these chairs. The cradle your father made for me has held many babies over many years, and I know this chair is solid and will last generations as well. And as you said, Vaice, there is a benefit to creating less expensive pieces so more people can enjoy the quality and beauty of the work."

"Thank you," Vaice said.

"However," Syrriah went on, "it's also true that the Carver name is know for intricate, unique pieces, and there will always be people who want those as well. My sugges-tion is that you divide the business into two businesses, both operating under the same name to remind buyers of the underlying quality, but clearly distinct in what products each business offers. Traditional methods on one side, new experiments on the other."

She felt a weight lift from her chest, leaving behind an almost giddy feeling. She didn't want to laugh at the looks on their faces, however, as their expressions turned from stubborn to dawning realization and shared consideration.

"I think…" Eron said. "I think that might just work."

"I think it might," Vaice agreed. "We'll have to figure out the details, of course."

Syrriah tried to sneak out while they were talking, but they caught her before she left, thanking her profusely and trying to press a gift into her hands. In the end she relented and took toys from the basket for her niece and nephew.

Then, her step lighter than it had been, she went to find her family.

> We sing away the old year, and welcome
>   the new
> We sing of the past, and the winter so cold
> We open ourselves to who we'll become
> We sing of the future and the secrets it
>   holds.

THE BELLS on the bridles of three steeds—Cefylla, and Natalli and Benlan's Companions—jangled in the sunshine, a counterpart to the honks of the snow geese flying overhead. The weather had held, cold but bright, and Syrriah had enjoyed every moment with her family before she had to leave.

Just as she would enjoy every moment back at Collegium.

Going home reminded her of all she had loved, and still loved.

It had also reminded her that she was a different person now, and had more to love and experience and learn.

Counseling Vaice and Eron had shown her that she did have at least a strong foundation of fairness and mediation to build upon as she completed her studies and became a full-fledged Herald.

:You see, my dove? I knew I Chose well.:

Syrriah leaned forward, hugging Cefylla's neck. *:Thank you, dearheart.:*

They rode together toward Syrriah's bright future.

"WHO WE'LL BECOME" takes place in author Mercedes Lackey's fantasy world of Valdemar. The story first appeared in the anthology *Choices: All-New Tales of Valdemar*, and is reprinted here with permission of Ms. Lackey.

A WITCH IN TIME

Dana

The kitchen of my Tudor-style house smelled of ginger and cinnamon and cloves, thanks to the cookies in the oven and the ones cooling on the racks, nearly ready for decorating. I opened my box of cookie cutters, each season's or holiday's cutters organized in their own, smaller boxes, and pulled out the ones for the Winter Solstice.

Stars (five-pointed stars are pentagrams, dammit, no matter what the non-pagans think), pine trees (we had them first, dammit), bells to ring in the growing light (ahem, dammit), mistletoe, and of course holly and oak leaves to symbolize the two Kings who would battle on Solstice Night.

The kitchen had oak beams on the ceiling, a rounded-top, Gothic-arch-carved door leading to the dining room, a white porcelain double-farmhouse sink, and a proper British Aga. Far better than those stainless steel monstrosities.

My pre-cog ability told me the cookies were ready a few seconds before the timer, so I was already sliding the tray out of the oven when the chime went off.

I slid the cookies onto a cooling tray, hung up my William Morris–patterned oven mitts, and hung my Good Housewitching apron on a hook. Time to collect my daughter, Ember, for the annual decorating fest.

Normally our coven, or at least some of us, would get together for the job (nobody had kitchen space for all thirteen of us), but this year was special. Ember had turned fifteen, and was ready to be welcomed into the coven to officially learn our ways.

I knocked on her door, and heard her muffled response to come in.

She lounged on her white-metal twin bed in a pair of heather-grey leggings and an oversized dark red sweater that draped almost to the ends of her fingers. White earbuds. Burgundy wool socks with hedgehogs on them.

She had my features—sharp cheekbones, enormous blue eyes, and hair that naturally fell in ringleted curls, only hers were long and currently piled atop her head, whereas I kept mine shoulder length—but she had her father's height.

Given that I was small and slender, people often told me I looked like a fairy, a notion I immediately dispelled when I opened my mouth. I curse like a drunken Scottish warlock (sometimes even with the accent).

People don't expect that.

"Time for cookie decorating!" I said.

Without looking up from her phone, Ember tapped her earbuds to turn them off and said, "No thanks."

I blinked. What the Goddess?

"But it's special this year," I said. "Just you and me, so we can talk about things."

By *things* I meant details of her entry into the coven, which she already knew was coming.

She sat up, rearranging herself so she was sitting cross-legged. "It's not that I don't respect your religion, Mom..." she began.

Hold on. *My* religion?

I should've expected something like this, but I'd accepted her excuses the past few weeks: studying for finals, holiday concert practice, a couple of parties.

But now it was the holiday break....

She shrugged dramatically, with a sigh and roll of her head. Of course she did. Find me a teenager, and I'll find you someone who shrugs dramatically.

"What do you think we do on the Sabbats and Esbats?" I tried. "Why we light candles, leave out offerings, bless the house for protection?"

"Mom, c'mon," she said. "What you and your friends do —it's just Witchcore."

"Witchcore?"

"Like Cottagecore, or Normcore, or Cabincore. It's an aesthetic. Decorating and clothes and candles and 'spells'."

I could hear the quote marks around "spells." I stiffened.

"It's more than that," I said.

"It's just an esthetic with magical icing on top," she said. "So you can tell who's at the door before they knock and keep lasagne from burning." She shrugged. "You won't even use whatever it is to clean the house or make things easier. You certainly don't use it to make the world a better place."

Even as my ire rose, I realized where she was coming

from. As the rest of us had with our children, as my own mother had done with me, I'd deliberately kept her innocent of the responsibilities and duties of being a witch. I'd wanted her to have a childhood—a certain amount of innocence, I suppose—before I burdened her.

That was what today was supposed to begin. An initiation, albeit a gentle one, into what being a witch really meant.

"You think we don't use our powers for good?"

"Sure, sometimes you help others, but really, what's the point? I'd rather do hands-on charity work. I'm already stuffing envelopes and stuff at Planned Parenthood."

My little do-gooder. She'd always been kind, since kindergarten when she took all the kids who were scared or crying under her wing.

Unfortunately, when she defended the less-strong, she had a habit of, er, using some of my words. The talk about her swearing with the teacher and principal had *not* been fun.

"You can do both, you know," I said.

"Look at your friends," Ember continued, ignoring me. "Having a feud over who decorates for the Solstice better. Last year's party was *so* embarrassing."

Philippa's entry to our neighborhood and coven had been rocky. She and my best friend, Kimberly, had gone head-to-head over who was the best at, well, pretty much everything. From holiday gifts to decorating to hosting parties, and more.

There had been a kerfluffle at the annual holiday party at Kimberly's when it turned out Philippa had "borrowed" Kimberly's coveted family fudge recipe.

Ember wasn't wrong. It hadn't been pretty.

The energy of their simmering feud blew up at the

Winter Solstice ritual, when the Oak and Holly king life-sized figures on Kimberly's roof came alive with the spirits of the two Gods. Kimberly and Philippa had to work together without anger to calm everything down.

They were cautious friends now, still negotiating who got to do what, and when. Philippa, for example, got Samhain as one of her holidays to shine, while Kimberly had the Winter Solstice to reign over.

I cleared my throat. "Is this something you've been thinking about long?"

"Isla and I have been talking," she said. "She thinks the same thing."

Isla was Ember's best friend and Philippa's daughter.

Ah, I understood what was going on. Ember was a teenager. She was finding her own path, and finding like-minded allies.

Ember—and Isla, apparently—just didn't have all of the information they needed.

I could sit Ember down and explain everything—but if she had given this so much thought, her reaction would be to dig in and double down. She wouldn't hear what I tried to tell her, tried to explain.

I had to handle this a different way.

"Okay," I said. "For now. We'll talk again, okay?"

Ember shrugged, but gave me a smile before she popped her earbud back in.

I knew she and I weren't in the right place to deal with this.

I knew I had to call in the big guns.

But first I was going to call Philippa to warn her that she would probably be having to deal with Isla, if she hadn't already.

At the back of the house we had an attached conservatory. More Victorian than Tudor, it was pentagonal, a story and a half tall, made of glass with black iron supports. It brimmed with plants: herbs both medicinal and culinary, hanging pots of trailing ivy, and urns filled with holly and lady's mantle and foxglove.

It was a cloudy mid-December day, but the room was warm and moist thanks to the plants. I breathed in the green, loamy, life-filled air.

I rolled back the rug in the center to reveal a large pentagram etched into the flagstone floor and painted a shimmering gold. I gathered five fat white candles from around the room and placed them at the points, then snapped my fingers to light them.

I settled myself in the middle of the star.

"You told me this day would come, Mom," I said with a sigh. "You cursed me with the 'just wait until you have a daughter' spell, and I'm sorry I didn't listen."

Then I began the ritual to have an oh-so-exciting chat with my deceased mother.

Ember

I woke suddenly, for a reason. Before I moved, I sent out feelers, inspecting the space around me. Mom had warded the house from negative energy (whatever that meant), but that didn't mean something couldn't go wrong.

Be wrong.

Something else here. I breathed in, out.

Sensed no bad intent.

Cautiously, I opened my eyes.

A hazy, glowing figure sat in my desk chair. I slowly sat up, and the figure resolved into a familiar form.

All of my tension melted away. "Grandma!"

"Ember, my sweet."

I didn't know how death worked, exactly; where people-slash-souls went, or how they came back occasionally. My grandmother looked younger than I remembered, or maybe just smoothed out. Fewer wrinkles, more youthful. Her pure white hair was plaited into a thick braid that fell over her shoulder, revealing silver earrings that were tiny windchimes. She wore jeans and a T-shirt that said "Styx" in a stylized font, although it didn't depict the river of Hades.

"Did Mom send you?" I asked as my sleep-fogged brain cleared.

"Now, why would you think that?" Grandma asked. "Can't a grandmother visit her granddaughter to check in?"

"You haven't 'checked in' since you died."

"Are you sure about that?" Grandma winked.

I remembered dreaming about my grandmother soon after she'd died, about how Grandma had so often sat at the foot of my bed, and in my dream I swear I'd *felt* the mattress depress.

And how I'd smelled my grandmother's special blend of wild rose, tobacco, and leather scent, like an old-fashioned gentleman's study—when no one was around.

Maybe they hadn't been dreams, exactly, after all.

"Okay, no," I confessed. "But why now?"

Grandma drummed her fingers on the arm of the chair.

"I need to show you some things. About our family, and our history. I could tell you, but it wouldn't be the same as seeing it."

I narrowed my eyes. "Which means what, exactly?"

"Well...how familiar are you with *Doctor Who*?"

"Not time theory." I groaned. "I hate time theory. It makes my head hurt."

"One way of looking at it is that time is a river. We step out and stand in the river at any point we choose...."

I groaned again and clutched my head.

Grandma considered, then gestured at the floor. The socks I'd toed off before bed, three shoes, one shirt, my tablet, my game controller, and a chair all moved out of the way, leaving an open area. Another wave of her hand, and a glowing golden circle appeared on the wooden planks.

Like the One Ring, but without the fancy Elven script. This one had symbols at the four quarters—the two solstices and two equinoxes—and in between each quarter —the four cross-quarter days.

The pagan Wheel of the Year.

"Go ahead, stand in the middle."

This was familiar; it was how we celebrated the year. When we created a ritual space, we turned in all four directions to call spirits or guardians of those quarters. I stepped inside, facing the Winter Equinox—we were close enough to that date. Nothing happened. I looked at my grandmother.

Granma flicked a finger, and the circle began to move deosil, or clockwise, turning in the direction of the sun. "See? You're the center. You don't move. The Wheel moves around you. Time moves around you. When you're alive, it's really hard to see and understand."

"Tell me about it," I murmured. I felt a frisson of energy traveling up from the earth and into me. I was grounding automatically, without thinking about it. I let the energy move through me and out the top of my head. It sort of made sense, but only if I didn't think about it too hard.

"Those of us who've moved on can grok it, though. And use it."

The circle stopped moving and faded into the floor.

"Come along," Grandma said, holding out her hand. "We're off on our magical mystery tour."

"Our *what* now?"

She stopped in her tracks and rolled her eyes. "Sweet Goddess. Your lack of musical knowledge is appalling. When we get back, I'm going to have words with your mother."

～

Ember

I found myself in space—or what looked like space. Blackness all around, pricked with pinpoints of glittering white light. I made the mistake of looking down and involuntarily clutched my grandmother's hand, then cursed myself for it.

Both for the clutching and the mistake of looking down.

We weren't standing on anything. I still felt as if I were standing, but it looked as though we were floating in the midst of the sky.

I didn't feel air on my skin, but I was somehow breathing. I was thankful there was no real smell, except something she could maybe describe as freshness. Like crisp, cold winter air.

Just not cold, or warm. Neutral.

Then, to make things worse, the stars began to move. Space *rotated*, which it just shouldn't do. Deosil, like the Wheel of the Year. My stomach lurched.

"Take a deep breath," Grandma said. "Another. There you go."

The nausea subsided. Although I still didn't look down again, or up. I decided to pretend I was in a planetarium, even though they made me dizzy and nauseated sometimes, too.

"Time," Grandma said. "We're in the center of it, as it moves around us."

"If you say so," I murmured. Speaking, I worried, would make my stomach somersault again.

"So like I said, I'm going to show you some things," Grandma said. "Ready?"

"Do I have a choice?" I asked, but my grandmother was already raising her free hand and making a slashing-down motion.

A crack appeared in front of us, and pure white light poured out. I barely had time to shield my eyes before Grandma tugged me along again, stumbling, this time through the rend.

~

Ember

We were in what looked like a courtroom, only old. A middle-aged woman stood behind a half-height dark wood wall, her hands resting on the edge. She was clearly wearing a corset, and over it a high-necked black dress. Her dark blond hair was pulled back, nothing fancy. A working-class woman.

Even from here I could see the exhaustion in her posture, the drawn skin around her mouth, her very energy.

"We can watch, but we can't interact," Grandma said. "No one can hear or see us. Probably a safety measure so we don't destroy life as we know it."

Which also explained why my pajamas and her jeans

weren't freaking anyone out.

"I get that part. Step on a butterfly, yadda yadda. But I know about the Salem Witch Trials," I said, sighing. "Ergot poisoning—not witchcraft or devil worship or magic."

"Seriously?" Grandma said. "Pay attention. Does this look like sixteen-nineties Massachusetts to you?"

Oh. No, actually, it did not.

Assumption, my mother was fond of saying, makes an ass out of you and me. I think she just enjoyed saying the word "ass." It was tame compared to some of her vocabulary.

I flushed, ashamed for jumping to conclusions.

"Nineteen...hundreds?" I guessed.

"Well done. Nineteen-oh-five, England. The woman on trial is a midwife. At this time, midwifery was legal per the Midwives Act of 1902, but..."

Grandma sighed. "No, this needs to start earlier. The Bible passage about not suffering a witch to live is a gross mistranslation. Long story short—"

"Thank you," I muttered under my breath. Not quietly enough, because she shot me a look that, if there were any energy behind it, would have turned me into a frog. Or a puddle for a frog.

"As I was *saying*, women were the first health practitioners. They knew herbs and how to make poultices, things we lost for a long time. Know why toothpaste is mint-flavored?"

"Tasty?" I ventured.

"Soothes the stomach," she said.

"Like after-dinner mints." I felt proud of myself for that.

"Wafer-thin mint?" she asked in a lilting voice.

"*What?*" I said.

"Your mother...your education..." she sputtered. She

waved her hands dismissively. "I'll deal with her later. My point is that women knew how mint and ginger were good for digestion, and feverfew eases headaches, and valerian is useful for pain relief...you get the idea. Thousands of years of women knowing what the eff they were doing, and then men create the field of medicine and codify it into a course of study that women aren't even *allowed* to take, and they decide that herbalism is dangerous because they don't believe in it and letting blood is oh so much better, and..."

She was getting worked up. I put a hand on her arm. "Careful, Grandma. Don't give yourself a heart attack."

"I'm dead, Ember. I don't have a beating heart, technically."

"Still," I said.

"Right. Men decided that women didn't know diddly squat, and the original bit in the Bible was about poisoners, which got translated to herbalists, which got translated to witches. And here, in the early nineteen hundreds, doctors didn't like that women preferred midwives—other women who understood exactly what childbirth felt like—over their lack of bedside manner. So they decided midwifery had to be official. A woman who wanted to be a midwife had to do three months of training and notify her intention to continue practicing annually."

"And this is relevant how?" I asked. "I mean, *are* they all witches?"

"Many of them, yes," Grandma said. "Herbal knowledge comes from earth-based energy. Adding a boost of magic can't hurt when it comes to healing somebody."

I looked down at the woman on trial. "And her? Why is she on trial?"

My grandmother shook her head. "Officially? Not being a registered midwife—she tried, but her reading skills weren't enough to get her through the training. But let's be honest: doctors didn't like that midwives—registered or not—helped destitute women...."

"Got it," I said. Destitute women who couldn't afford another mouth to feed.

"Okay, so witches were persecuted," I said, feigning boredom even though my heart ached for the woman on trial. (Even though I knew she was long dead, it felt real, here, now.) "I already knew that."

My grandmother sighed again, took my hand, yanked me back through a rift into the spinning stars, then through another....

What followed was what I'd call the dreaded montage if this were a movie. Brief glimpses of a variety of cultures and places, women (and sometimes men) worshipping, healing, casting circles and drawing energy and doing things I didn't recognize except to understand it was all related.

"Paganism, Wicca, the Old Ways. Druidism," Grandma's voice echoed in my head. "In other countries, Norse mythology, Greco-Roman, Asian, what have you. It's not about a belief in a god, or multiple gods, or god-excuse explanations of the world, but the relationship with the earth, air, fire, water. The patterns of the world. Intuition. Deep knowledge."

I couldn't deny it: the words "deep knowledge" struck something deep inside of me, resonated. Maybe—okay, I would deny this out loud—brought tears to my eyes.

Then we were dropping into more recent times. My grandmother, fighting to make paganism an official religion. The success when it was recognized by the US military. Witches around the world connecting at the same time to give healing strength on Earth Day.

And then, last year.

My mother and her best friend, Kimberly, in Kimberly's kitchen, as Kimberly complained about Philippa.

"Jealousy is a negative emotion, and it'll suck away your energy if you let it continue," my mother told her.

Now in our own plant-filled sunroom, my mother with a group of her friends, and one of them, Maggie, saying to Kimberly, "Everyone has different strengths and weaknesses."

But then we were outside, pre-dawn, and my mother and Philippa were both creeping around through the snow, depositing baked delicacies and other gifts at all the houses in the neighborhood.

"The argument between Kimberly and Philippa was, in many ways, about who could give more," Grandma said. "Sure, Kimberly had always been the one to do all this, and Philippa challenged her standing in the community, and yes, things got out of hand. Nobody's perfect, especially when there's a clash of strong personalities."

I couldn't think of anything to say to that.

Another montage, showing me that Mom and the coven also delivered tins of cookies and treats to emergency rooms and fire stations and police stations every year on Christmas Eve, New Year's Eve, the Fourth of July—times when workers couldn't be home with their families, when accidents and injuries were at their worst.

Those goodies, Grandma told me, were imbued with strength and hope, so that the people on the front lines could keep going.

And then there were the gifts delivered to local hospital wards.

I deny that I shed any tears then. Do not push me.

Then we had one final stop in time....

My mother, in town on a sunny autumn day, her cloth

shopping bags bulging as she walked back to her car. Suddenly, she froze. Her head whipped around.

Then she dropped the groceries, ran down the sidewalk, and pulled a kid back from stepping into the road, even though no cars were visible.

The car whipped around the corner a few seconds later.

My mother and her friends *did* use their abilities to make the world a better place. Not by any grand gestures.

By one person at a time.

Message received.

I cursed in a way that would make my mother proud.

Or not.

～

Ember

Then we were back in my bedroom. I glanced out the window. It was still dark, still night.

"I brought you back to seconds after we left," Grandma said.

I was exhausted. I kissed Grandma on the cheek, fell onto my bed, and despite how my brain was whirling with everything I'd seen, I was out before I could even burrow under the covers.

～

Dana

"Good morning," I said cautiously when Ember stumbled blearily into the kitchen. I slid a heavy white mug of coffee—cream, three sugars—across the counter to her, because, of course, I'd known she was about to walk in.

Her blond curls were tangled and her pajamas looked

more than slept in.

"Thanks," she said by way of greeting. She slid onto a kitchen stool, took the mug in both hands, and drank deeply.

"How are you?" I asked cautiously.

"You sicced dead Grandma on me," she said, lowering the mug and glaring at me. "She says she's going to have words with you about music and wafer-thin mints."

I stared at her. I hadn't expected that *at all*.

She shrugged. "I didn't get it, either."

"Did...your grandmother have anything else to say?"

She buried her face in her mug. When she reemerged, she looked more like herself. Caffeine. So magical, you'd think witches invented it.

She took a deep breath. "I'm sorry for what I said yesterday. I didn't understand everything, and I think I have a better grasp now."

"Apology accepted," I said. "I'm sorry I didn't explain enough earlier."

She nodded, and set the mug down carefully. "After I shower, I'd like to bake cookies with you." She didn't look up until the end of her sentence, as if afraid of what my reaction would be.

I tried to keep myself from full-on beaming, because I knew that would provoke at eye roll, at the very least. "I'd like that, too," I said.

"Can I invite Isla?"

"If it's all right with her mother."

She slid off the stool and hugged me. Best feeling in the world, even if she *was* taller than me.

I watched her leave the kitchen.

It was time for my little witchling to learn what she could do.

CHRISTMAS EVE AT CLAREDON HALL

F rigid rain slashed down at me from every direction. The variable gusts of lashing wind made it impossible to predict from which direction the next onslaught of water would come: into my face, or down the back of my neck, no matter how many times I pulled my collar up and close. My brimmed hat was next to useless, just becoming something else I had to clutch on to with numbed fingers, along with my medical bag.

England would not see a white Christmas tomorrow.

No souls, hardy or not, should be out on a foul night like this, I thought dourly, my boots slipping in the mud of the wooded path I could barely make out in the darkness. But as the soon-to-be-installed doctor in the town, the duty fell to me—my elderly, soon-to-be predecessor was in no shape to make the journey to Claredon Hall on a howling, stormy night like this.

I'd already heard tales of Claredon Hall and its inhabitants. In towns like this, information (gossip) is bestowed like gold from a benevolent king.

One who desires your favor.

Up ahead I could hear the crashing of Monkshead River. Even in clement weather, it was a fast-running current through dangerous outcroppings of rock. Now, swollen by rain, it sounded like an angry, howling monster.

So intent was I on not slipping and falling in the mud nor missing the crossing that I neither saw nor heard the other man approaching until he was almost upon me. I skidded to a stop as he said, his voice raised to carry over the wind and water, "Well met on this ill night, sir. I hope I did not startle you."

Willing my pounding heart to slow, I peered through the rain at him. Dark hair plastered to his head and face, a face barely visible in the gloom. I couldn't make out his clothing, although somehow, I sensed he was a soldier. Perhaps something in his bearing. Either way, he didn't look or sound familiar, so someone I hadn't encountered in town yet.

"Only so far as I didn't expect another foolhardy soul to be out in this abysmal storm," I said.

"Only foolhardy souls who fear disappointing a loved one on Christmas more than a cold dousing, I suspect," he said.

"Or foolhardy souls whose profession stops for no weather." I touched my hat with my freezing hand. "Bertram Pierce, incoming town physician."

He nodded his sodden head. "Well met, sir."

"I'm headed to Claredon Hall," I added. "I hope I haven't missed the turnoff for the bridge."

"Indeed you haven't," he said. "Claredon Hall, hm? I..."

He shook his head, but began walking with me as I started out again, for I had no desire to dilly-dally until I turned into ice and shattered.

"You're familiar with Claredon Hall?" I prompted, not

pressing for information, but trying to start a conversation to take my mind away from the miserable night.

"Oh yes," he said. "Quite. What brings you there on this frightful night?"

"An illness," I said. "One of the older folks."

I didn't elaborate, for that would be skirting too close to client privilege, even though I wouldn't know what the illness was until I examined Lady Shaw.

Claredon Hall, I'd been told more than once, had fallen on hard times over the past few years. Oh, the Shaws were still a generous and caring family, and they weren't destitute, not really. But poor investments, and the war, had eaten into the family fortune. The sons had gone on to banking or law—respectable professions, although somewhat looked-down-upon ones for those of higher birth. The eldest daughter, married. The family had closed off some of the house, it had been explained to me in hushed voices, and kept only a bare staff now of butler, housekeeper, one or two maids, a groundskeeper....

With the older sons and daughter away, the household consisted of the current Lord and Lady Shaw, a daughter, and a maiden aunt—the Lady Millicent Shaw I would be attending to if I made it there unscathed.

I should have called on them earlier as a matter of propriety, but I simply hadn't had the opportunity. Then the request for a doctor's visit had reached our office.

The roar of Monkshead River was louder now, and as I squinted through the rain, I thought I saw the path to take me to the bridge.

"I believe this is the way I must go," I said. I turned toward the direction of the sound. Over the bridge, and onto Claredon Hall land, with a direct route up the lawn to the manor.

My step almost lightened at the thought of being nearly there.

A hand seized upon my arm. "Wait!"

I spun around. The other man's eyes were wide beneath his water-soaked hair, the pupils dark as the night around us.

Before I could respond, he gasped, "The bridge...the bridge is out. It always goes out when the river gets this high. You won't be able to see until it's too late."

I sagged at the thought of turning around, fighting my way back through the woods and the storm, failing at my mission.

"There's another bridge upstream," he said. "Not terribly far. It's safer."

I was trusting a stranger, but I didn't see much choice, not if I was going to have a chance of examining Miss Shaw, which was my duty and responsibility.

He was correct: it wasn't terribly far until the next bridge, which I could see was intact, higher over the water than apparently the other was.

"Cross here, head left around the lake, then up to the house," he said. "Watch your footing; it'll be slippery."

"You're not headed this way as well?" I asked. As far as I knew, there were no other homes or villages in this direction for some way. Surely the Shaws would take him in for the night.

"I have..." he hesitated "...an appointment I cannot miss."

At another time I might have pressed him further, but I had been requested by the Shaws for medical purposes, and they were my priority. Plus I needed to get inside before I caught my own death from the chill.

As much as I owed him for his suggestion of a detour that might very well have saved my life.

"My thanks to you, then," I said. "I wish you nothing but the best." I turned towards the river, but over the roar I heard him call, "One more thing, please."

And again I turned back, blinking against the deluge.

"Might I beg a boon of you?" he asked. His voice shook. "Would you deliver a letter for me, to Miss Shaw? I'm not sure...I'm not sure I will make it there tonight."

"Of course," I said. "It's the least I can do."

He pressed an envelope into my hand, and I shoved it deep into my coat pocket, as far away from the rain as I could manage.

When I looked up again, he was gone, dissolved into the driving rain and night-dark forest.

On the wide wooden bridge, I looked down at the churning, frothing water, tumbling endlessly against the rocks, and could not help but suppress a shudder.

I RANG the bell of Claredon House. I couldn't see much of it in the storm, though I could tell that it was made of local pale yellow stone and had several wings spreading out from the solid front. Georgian modification, I guessed, from an earlier building.

The door opened.

The butler's uniform was a bit shiny at the cuffs, and the butler himself was an older man, receding pale hair going white at the temples. But his straight-backed, solid mien and the slightest of scowls showed he was a man who took his duties seriously indeed.

"May I help you?" he asked, as if it were a common

occurrence to find a drenched man on the doorstep on Christmas Eve.

"Doctor Pierce, here at the behest of Lord Shaw," I said. "I'm here to see Miss Shaw?"

"Have I heard my name?" came a voice from within. A lilting female voice.

The butler stepped aside and ushered me in with a small gesture. I entered, resisting the urge to shake my coat collar away from my sodden neck.

Stepping inside was almost a shock, especially the relative silence when the butler closed the door again the drumming of the rain. The two-story foyer was lit and warm and quiet, its pale yellow wallpaper bringing a hint of light against the darkness outside. To my right, a grand staircase swept up, the mahogany balustrade adorned with sweetly scented pine boughs.

The speaker with the melodious voice came into view.

She had chestnut-brown hair pulled back in a popular style, although her evening dress was several years out of fashion. (I had a sister who spoke knowingly about such things; I had given up protesting that I had no interest.) She had a strong nose and kind, intelligent hazel eyes. A dimple in her left cheek—a cheek flushed from, no doubt, the fire in the parlor—flashed as she smiled and held out her hand.

"I'm Miss Larissa Shaw."

I touched my fingertips to hers, nodded my head, and said, "I am pleased to make your acquaintance. But I fear I'm not here to see you, but one Miss Millicent Shaw."

"My great-aunt. Of course. You must be Doctor Pierce."

The butler cleared his throat. It had been his duty to introduce me. She smiled at him as well, and thanked him.

"If you could find Doctor Pierce some clean clothes— something of my father's should fit him, please," she added. "Then go back to your festivities, and I'll ring you if anything is needed."

He could tell by the struggle on his face that he wanted to protest, but he said, "Thank you, your ladyship," and retreated.

"Now," she said, looking at me again. "You're drenched. Granger will procure some of father's clothes. Come to the fire to warm yourself—you must be chilled to the bone."

She kindly didn't draw notice to my soiled trousers (I'd lost my footing on my way up the sloped, slippery lawn, scraping away the grass and landing with both knees in the mud).

I tried to demur, to insist that my patient required priority, but she would have none of it.

"Great-Aunt Millie is ill, yes, but she was down for supper a few hours ago. She can wait a few moments. If you fall ill, you'll be no use to any of your patients."

So I allowed myself to be warmed by the parlor fire while we waited for Granger to return. I met Lord and Lady Shaw, Lady Larissa's parents. He was a wide-shouldered man with a strong voice, and she was elegant and courteous. A crystal glass containing two fingers of whiskey was pressed into my hands, and I accepted it as a medicinal to assist me in warming up. My first priority was to stop shivering.

Granger showed me to a cloakroom where I changed into the dry clothing (a bit snug in some places and loose in others), after which I insisted on seeing the patient.

"Follow me," Lady Larissa said, and of course I had no option but to do so.

"Every year just before Christmas, my great-aunt insists on walking the grounds, no matter the weather," she said as we headed up the grand staircase. The scent of pine filled my nose, bringing memories of Christmases past. "As you've seen, this year has been particularly bad, and she's caught a chill."

"Why does she do this? Walk the grounds, I mean."

Lady Larissa sighed. I stopped and looked at her, and saw a sadness in her hazel eyes. "Great-Aunt Millie was engaged to a man who went to war. He swore he'd be home for Christmas—she'd had correspondence from him confirming that he was alive and well, out of danger, and on his way."

"But he didn't arrive," I guessed.

"No. On Christmas Day, Wilifred, Earl of Spotswood, visited with the news that Great-Aunt Millie's fiancé had perished, not in the war, but by losing his step and plunging into the Monkshead River. His body had been found downriver, battered by the rocks."

"Your poor great-aunt," I said. "And the poor man, to have survived so much, only to…"

"Quite tragic," Lady Larissa agreed. "The curious thing was, he knew this land like the back of his hand, having grown up nearby. Even though there was a terrible storm that night—I suspect as wild a night as this one—one would think he would have known what to expect."

We walked along a dark-paneled corridor. There was a fine film of dust on the plate rail. The scent of pine receded, replaced by the subtle rosewater scent Lady Larissa carried.

I cleared my throat. "Other than her holiday wanderings, how is your great-aunt's health?"

"Fit as a fiddle, really. She rarely falls ill."

In an effort to be delicate, I had made my question too vague. "I mean…her mental acuity."

"Oh, goodness!" Lady Larissa laughed shortly. "Even

fitter than a fiddle. She has retained her sharp wit, and she can usually beat anyone at Whist or Dictionary."

Her sudden, unfettered laugh brought warmth to my limbs where the fire had not.

We found Lady Millicent in her bed—one with walnut barley-twist posts—propped up by pillows, a lace nightcap on her head, an alcoholic nightcap on her table, and a book in her hand.

I could tell that she was a hardy soul, but Lady Millicent's cheeks were flushed like Lady Larissa's, even though the room was cooler, despite the fire crackling sweetly in the hearth. And for Lady Millicent, it was because she had a fever. Her eyes, hazel like Larissa's, were bright. But brighter than they ought to be.

Beneath her cap, her hair was iron-gray, and the wrinkles around her mouth and eyes blossomed when she smiled at me.

"You came all this way, in the storm, for me?" she asked, her voice husky but without quaver. "I am quite grateful, although I imagine there's little you can do. I'll be fine after a wee nip of whiskey and honey, and a good sleep." She had to pause between phrases to draw in air.

"I have no doubt that you will, Lady Millicent," I said. It was a gentle lie, one I had been taught at medical college. "But your nephew requested me, and here I am."

I asked her a few questions regarding coughing, breathing, and chest pain, then listened to her lungs. Through my stethoscope I heard the distinctive crackle both I'd expected and feared.

Pneumonia.

I prescribed a dose of opium in her nightcap, and in her tea in the mornings; I'd brought enough with me for several days, thankfully. I counseled that she should take a daily hot bath—twice, if she could.

There was little else I could do. Previous doctors might have suggested leeches or other methods of draining fluid from the body, but I held no stock with that nonsense.

Despite my concerns, she seemed otherwise in fine constitution, and it was as likely as not that a few days of rest and my prescriptions would bring her back to full health.

"I'll leave you to your rest," I said, and opened my bag to return my stethoscope.

Then I saw the envelope, the one the man in the woods had entrusted to me. I had transferred it from the pocket of my sodden coat (now likely hung in the laundry below-stairs to dry) to my bag when I changed.

"One more thing," I said. "I met a man on my way here who asked me to deliver a letter to you."

Her sparse eyebrows rose. "To me?"

"To Miss Millicent Shaw," I said, just as was scripted on the envelope.

The flush on her face deepened, and her blue-veined hand trembled as she took the envelope from my hand. The flap parted easily, no doubt because of the paper's damp-ness. She drew out several small sheets of paper. The blue ink had bled a little, even inside.

She held the letter out to Lady Larissa. "Please, dear, would you?"

Given that she had been reading a book when we entered, I wondered how bad her eyesight was...until it occurred to me later that as the tale unfolded, perhaps she had known she needed witnesses—or companions—to help her bear the revelations within.

"Of course," Lady Larissa said, smoothing out the pages

with slender fingers and lifting the first to the gas lamp on the wall so she could see more clearly.

My dearest Millie,

I can call you that, because we're betrothed, and no one else has to see this letter. You are mine, and I am yours, forever and beyond, as we've always said.

"Forever and beyond," Lady Shaw repeated softly, nodding.

I promised I would be home by Christmas, as by God, I nearly was. So close. I departed the train in town to a miserable storm on Christmas Eve, but I wouldn't let a little rain and wind to keep me from my beloved girl, not when I'd promised.

I could see you, dearest Millie, standing on the lawn, your lantern held high to guide me to you. So intent was I on the sight of that lantern—and you—that I failed to noticed the gap in the bridge.

But it wasn't your fault, my Millie girl, please don't think that for a moment. No, just before I set foot on the bridge, I encountered...

"Encountered whom?" Lady Millicent demanded when Lady Larissa fell silent.

"I'm afraid the ink didn't survive the rain, Great-Aunt. Let me continue and we'll see if we can't piece it together afterwards."

"Go on, then, child."

...who said that he'd just crossed the bridge and all was well.

My dearest, you are mine and I am yours, forever and beyond. Know that I loved you in this life and still love you after. You are my light and my heart.

Yours forever
and with much fondness,
Bertie

Lady Millicent wordlessly held out her hand, and Lady Larissa handed back the pages. Lady Millicent pressed them to her bosom.

"Thank you. Thank you." Her eyes were bright now with brimming tears as she reached out with her other hand to grasp on of mine. "I can't tell you much this means to me. He was coming home. I knew he was coming home to me."

As a man of science, despite all the evidence—the man I met who I guessed was a soldier, the story the ladies Millicent and Larissa told—it had not occurred to me until now (and even now doubt warred with what I was hearing) that the supernatural might be involved.

Despite the room's fire, despite the dry clothes I'd been given and the whisky that had warmed me from within, I shuddered.

"He says he encountered someone on his way here," Lady Larissa mused. "Were there any guests here that evening, Great-Aunt?"

"We don't usually entertain on Christmas Eve," Lady Millicent said. "Only family."

"Yet here I am," I said lightly.

Suddenly she sat upright, which brought on a fit of coughing. She pressed a lace-edged handkerchief to her mouth, and Lady Larissa was quick to offer her some tea when the spate had ended.

"There was someone here that evening," Lady Millicent said after sipping. "Lord Spotswood." Her mouth twisted in a moue of distaste. "He was once again trying to persuade me to accept his proposal of marriage."

"But you were engaged to Albert," Lady Larissa said.

"Oh, he knew that very well, but he felt Albert was

beneath me." She shook her head. "I wouldn't have said yes to Lord Spotswood if he were the last man left in England. I once witnessed him kick one of his hunting dogs so hard, the poor thing had to be put down. He was a loathsome, vile man."

A thought occurred to me, and I asked to see the letter. When it was in my hands I held it up to the lamp, examining the spot where the ink had run and blurred.

My profession had gifted me with an unlikely talent, that of deciphering poor handwriting and cryptic notations.

"It's possible," I said slowly, "that the person your Albert encountered was Lord Spotswood."

Lady Larissa took the pages from me with a delicate, long-fingered hand, and perused the same spot. "I do believe you're right, Dr. Pierce." She raised her gaze to meet mine. Her eyes were a dusky hazel, not quite green, not quite brown. "Does that mean Lord Spotswood...?"

Her quick mind had latched on to what I had been thinking. "That he led Albert to his demise."

Lady Millicent's lips had paled as she pressed them together. "I am sorry to say, as much as the idea is repugnant, such a vile deed would not have been outside the realm of possibility for him." She shook her head slowly. "It would explain why he had been so keen to press for my hand on Christmas Eve."

"And where is Lord Spotswood now?" I asked. Despite my exhaustion from my trek through the storm, I felt a surge of chivalry, as if it had become my duty to confront the man about his potential misdeed decades earlier.

"Passed on, and no doubt damned straight to Hell's fires," Lady Millicent said. "Killed during a hunt when his horse threw him, then stepped on him." There was a dark glint in her eye when she added, "I've always imagined that horse was expressing an opinion, shall we say."

Neither Lady Larissa nor I had a response to that.

Lady Millicent sank back against her pillows, her complexion wan. The discussion had wearied her, when she was already battling illness. Lady Larissa said she would call for the nightcap, and I retreated downstairs with her to instruct the kitchen staff on the opium dosage.

Lord and Lady Shaw of course insisted I stay the night, and given the way the storm continued to rage outside, I had no desire to demur. A plate of food—left-over roasted goose and potatoes from their evening meal—had already been prepared for me. I hadn't realized how ravenous I was, but I ate as slowly as I could, for decorum's sake.

I thought I would have trouble falling asleep, my mind awhirl with the events of the evening. Had I indeed met a man in the woods? Had he indeed given me a letter from beyond the grave? I couldn't fathom it. And yet, how could I deny it?

The rain spattered like stones against the window at random intervals thanks to the changeable wind, causing me to jump at each rattle.

But the food and whiskey and warm bed, after I'd tired myself struggling through the miserable storm, had their effect, and I had no memory of dropping into sleep.

~

A BRIGHT SHAFT of sunlight woke me the next morning, finding a gap in the long drapes and resting itself across my slumbering eyelids. I rose and drew the drapes back. The sky, clear and pale blue, pretended there had been no storm. Indeed, the entire experience felt like something from a dream.

The grounds said otherwise. Slate shingles were shattered on the flagstone below me. The long gouges of my muddy footprints marred the once-manicured lawn, and the treeline was littered with fallen branches. A storm will always pass, but it will also always leave its mark behind.

I hadn't been awoken by a footman, not did I expect the family had one to spare, but when I turned from the window, I saw that my clothing hung on a valet stand. Even my hat was pressed, the brim sharp.

In the light, I could see the shabbiness in the corners of the room: the faded upholstery on one chair, the dust that had settled on the baseboards. Indeed, the bed linens last night had held a faint musty smell, but I had been far too exhausted to care. I was still grateful for the hospitality.

I dressed swiftly, as the fire was mere coals and the room had grown chill and I was shivering, and splashed my face in a basin of water before making my way downstairs.

Following voices, I found the family was in the breakfast room, except for the elder Lady Shaw.

Lord Shaw rose as I entered, holding his white linen napkin so it didn't slip from his lap. "Dr. Pierce. We thought you might appreciate not being woken early, given the late night you'd had. Happy holidays. Goodness, that was the worst storm we've had on Christmas Eve in fifty years."

"Please, join us," Lady Shaw said, indicating the polished oak buffet along one wall.

There were kippers and toast and eggs, sliced tomatoes and grilled mushrooms, and piping hot tea. The fanciful said tea, not blood, ran through the veins of a proper Englishman. As a physician, I knew better, but I couldn't deny how a bracing brew raised one's spirits.

"Thank you," I said. "I appreciate a warm meal before I take the walk back to the village. Although the storm has passed, it looks to be a cold day. I'll check on Lady Shaw before I depart, of course."

"Surely you can stay for luncheon," the younger Lady Shaw said with a pretty smile, a dimple accentuating her cheek. Her day dress today was a muted green that warmed her eyes, and her chestnut-brown hair gleamed.

"I'm afraid not," I said, returning her smile, mine albeit apologetic. "Despite the holiday, I do have duties to attend to."

The rest might well have been expected. When I went to check on Lady Millicent, I found her cold in her bed, a faint smile upon her face and the envelope against her breast.

I assured the family I would contact the coroner as soon as I returned to the village. Lady Larissa showed me to the door, tears sparkling on her pale, pretty cheeks.

I took her hands in mind. "In the light of day," I said, keeping my voice low, "are we sure of the events of last night? The letter...the letter could have been given to me by a relative of Lord Spotswood's—perhaps Lord Spotswood had deathbed remorse?"

"According to my great-aunt, Lord Spotswood died on the...died instantly," she said. "If you're questioning your experience, or from whom the letter came, well, 'There are more things in heaven and earth, Horatio, than are dreamt of in your philosophy.'"

I blinked. "You know Shakespeare."

That unfettered laugh burst forth again, albeit tempered and a bit shaky. "My parents believed we should all receive the same education, brothers and sisters alike. I'm well-versed in the bard along with many other subjects."

My esteem of Miss Shaw grew warmly in my chest.

And yet—and yet—to to agree with her theory went against everything I had learned and embraced.

And yet—and yet—could I deny my experiences from last night?

Granger's harrumph was almost silent, but nonetheless clear. I was taking liberties. I bowed my head, slid my hands away from hers, missing the warmth of her fingers.

Lady Larissa bade me a safe journey back and invited me to visit whenever I wished.

My reply was noncommittal as I touched my hat, gathered my bag, and took my leave.

I made my way cautiously down the sloping lawn, for the ground was still sodden, the mud slick beneath the grass.

Lady Larissa was a lovely young woman, and indeed I'd found myself taken with her. Her knowledge, her strength, and yes, her beauty.

But in the bright, cold light of Christmas Day, the previous evening's events seemed distant, a fever-dream. My studies, my training, all led to the immutable fact that ghosts did not exist, that spirits did not roam the land.

I was a doctor. A man of science. I understood reason and experiments and tangible evidence.

And yet, I could not deny the encounter I had had and the unearthly results.

I would have to reconcile all this within not only my brain, but my heart.

Because I also knew this: with all my heart, I wished to find every excuse to return to Claredon Hall.

DESPERATE HOUSEWITCHES

It started with the Samhain decorations.

It would get worse at Yule.

Much worse.

I just didn't know that yet.

"I just don't like her," I said between gritted teeth, furiously polishing a silver quaich, the shallow bowl with two stag's heads as handles that we needed for our Samhain ritual.

"Jealousy is a negative emotion, and it'll suck away your energy if you let it continue," Dana said reasonably.

Dana was my best friend; we'd grown up in this neighborhood together, taken over our respective mothers' places in the coven when it came time, brought in husbands and, in her case, started raising children. She was small and slender and looked like most people's idea of a fairy, with blond ringlets and impossibly wide blue eyes—an image that was shattered whenever she cursed, because she had a hell of a potty mouth.

She was my best friend and I loved her, even when she was right and I stubbornly refused to admit it.

We were in my house, a Gothic Victorian with a widow's walk (unnecessary in a neighborhood not remotely near the ocean, but still charming) and stained glass framing the windows. All the houses on our block are different styles, from Painted Ladies to Craftsman bungalows. There's even a black-beamed, white-stuccoed Tudor the next street over. Some people say our houses slowly conform to the owners.

They wouldn't be wrong.

The kitchen smelled like pumpkin and spices, which made sense, because I was baking for the ritual as well. Of course we'd have the traditional cakes and ale as part of the ceremony, but I also always made extra to send home with everyone.

"I'm *not* jealous," I said.

Dana pointed out the window, across the street to Philippa's house (Arts and Crafts Movement, and I happen to know it looked like William Morris had exploded inside). "You're telling me that you don't feel threatened that she's probably going to win Best Decorated House this year?"

Of *course* I felt threatened. I'd won Best Decorated House for the past ten years, ever since I set up residence here. In our coven, I was the one with the best decorations, the best food at potlucks, the best parties, the best poison garden (for show only, of course)...it was my *thing*. Everybody knew it was my thing, and everybody loved me for it.

And then Philippa had come to town. Pretty Philippa, with her stupid English accent and her high-and-mighty "I'm from England so I know how the rituals are really supposed to go" and her Goddess-damned *decorations*.

I put down the quaich and picked up the chalice of simple beaten silver. Before I attacked it with the polishing cloth, though, I closed my eyes and took a deep, cleansing breath. In through the nose, out through the mouth. Ground, center. If I let my negative energy seep into the tools, the Solstice ritual would go all wonky, and you did *not* want anything to go wrong at Samhain, when the Veil Between the Worlds was thinnest. No telling what might come through.

I could have used magic to polish the ritual tools—just like I could've used magic to keep my house clean and tidy, bake all the holiday goodies, grow my herbs and vegetables. (Okay, sometimes I encouraged the plants—but I still got my hands in the dirt and pulled all the weeds.) But that would be missing the point. Everything in life was Ritual, and you imbued your personal magic in it *as* you did the work. You didn't use magic *instead* of doing the work.

The meditation helped; I felt centered in what I was doing, knowing it was right. But as I commenced polishing, I couldn't help glancing out the window again, and I felt my blood pressure start to creep up again.

Philippa used magic for everything.

The maple trees outside Philippa's house seemed to be producing the brightest flaming leaves on the block—and even the leaves on the ground didn't seem to be losing their color, arranging themselves artfully, as if in a painting titled something twee like "Enchanted Autumn" or "Tree of Fire."

Ravens—real ones. How she convinced those ornery buggers to stick around, I don't know, and I wasn't about to admit they really added a certain something. Garlands of black oak leaves and a vase of black roses on the porch (possibly not real, but I wouldn't put it past her). Clusters of impossibly intricately carved jack o'lanterns. Purple and orange lights highlighted every window, every eave, lit and visible even during the day.

Meanwhile, just yesterday, she'd left baskets on everybody's porches, filled with homemade foods of the season: mulled wine and cider, tarts of pumpkin and apple, a thick, hearty stew and fresh bread. That was my *thing*, too, and Philippa had beaten me by one day. *One freaking day.* The gingerbread had been cooling on wire racks when Philippa had dropped off her basket.

She'd included aprons in each of our colors in the baskets. Last year, I'd delivered hand-embroidered dish towels. I figured I still won there.

I also had made adorable witch's hat fascinators to give out at the potluck, so there.

"Nobody loves you any less," Dana said. "Maybe it's okay for you to step back and let someone else have a little of the limelight. Maybe you can *relax* and not feel so much pressure to be perfect."

"I don't feel any pressure to be perfect," I protested, and I really didn't. "I *like* doing all this. And I like things just so. I like things organized and familiar." I knew I sounded just a skosh whiny when I added, "Philippa's messing everything up."

"She wouldn't've been able to move here if she didn't fit in with our core beliefs," Dana, ever logical, pointed out. "We all agreed."

"I didn't say she was a bad person, or a bad pagan," I said. "I said she was pissing me off."

Dana went to the oven and pulled out the pies about two seconds before the timer went off, because she had a bit of pre-cog ability.

"And I don't blame you for that," she said, her cheeks flushing from the heat. "But it seems like she's here to stay, and you're going to have to find a way to coexist with her."

I did the mental equivalent of sticking my fingers in my ears and chanting "I can't hear you."

Because for all our skill at divination, no witch can see the specifics of the future. (Remember, kids, prophecies are open to interpretation, and you're likely to pick the wrong one. So just don't go there.)

~

Philippa beat my hat fascinators with seasonal incense, specifically magicked for each of the thirteen of us. *And* she won Best Decorated House.

The ritual was a little strained, but nothing untowards happened.

It was uncharitable of me, and I knew it, but I still seethed. And plotted how to outdo her—outdo myself—at the Winter Solstice.

~

It started, again, with decorations.

Philippa snuck hers up in the middle of the night, it seemed, because December first dawned on evergreens (yes, she *changed what kinds of trees she had in her front yard*) draped in ropes of glowing snowflakes, and her house had garlands of holly and ivy, and huge lit-up holly and oak leaves in the wide front window. Holiday music emanated from her yard at all hours of the day and night—not loud or obnoxious, but the white lights that adorned her house and the trees blinked and shimmered with the beat.

Did I mention the smells? Pine and nutmeg and peppermint; you caught whiffs as you walked by. Not all at once, of course.

Then there was the horse. Philippa had told us all, more than once (ad nauseum), that her name meant "lover of horses" and that the horse was her spirit animal. So she'd put out a life-sized Hooden Horse with its companions: a groom with a whip, several musicians, and a man dressed in women's clothing. (The British seem to be big on the latter, if their holiday pantomimes are anything to go by.)

"From East Kent, apparently, but you see similar traditions in Caerleon, Wales, and Lancashire," Dana told me. She and I and our friend Maggie were in Dana's plant-filled sunroom—which felt sunny even though the glowering sky threatened more snow—drinking tea spiced with cloves and cinnamon and orange, and wrapping presents. I'd made cloth bags out of all my appropriate scrap fabric for the year, and was sorting bags to gifts based on size, and estimating how much cord I'd need to weave.

I paused to look at Dana, raising an eyebrow. I didn't even have to say anything.

"She told me about it when she had me over for coffee," Dana said. My eyebrow didn't waver. "I can visit her for coffee without betraying our friendship," Dana protested.

I didn't ask her whose house decorations she'd voted for at Samhain. I didn't want to know.

And yes, she was right: she could visit whomever she darn well wanted.

The Hooden Horse's wooden head was festooned with bells and rosettes. Its jaw was hinged, and it would crack shut at various intervals. According to my own research, the head on a pole was traditionally carried around the big houses of the parish just before Christmas.

What*ever*.

I'd gone with more familiar, traditional decorations, with lights shaped like pentagrams (what, you never noticed that people hang five-pointed stars at the holidays?), big pots of poinsettias (spelled to not be poisonous to neighborhood critters), and life-sized models of the Oak King and the Holly King battling it out on the roof.

How is that not traditional? The Winter Solstice is the longest night of the year, a time when the two Gods (or two aspects of the same God, depending on who you follow) duke it out. The winter Holly King dies to give the next half of the year over to the summer Oak King, which allows the days to start growing longer again. At the Summer Solstice, they'd repeat their fight, and the Holly King would reign again.

Anyway, it was funny that I never saw Philippa put up those middle-of-the-night decorations, given that I had been creeping around the neighborhood at the very same time, hanging mistletoe on everyone's porches.

Yes, I used a little magic so I didn't leave footprints in the snow. So sue me.

"Everyone has different strengths and weaknesses," Maggie said. Her hair had gone pure white when she was in her twenties, and between that and her willowy height and green eyes, she was incredibly striking. She was principal at the local grade school, where she put the fear of the Goddess in all the little children.

"And my weakness is competitiveness; I get it," I said.

"No," Maggie said. "It's not a weakness. You two have to find a way to get along, sure, but it takes two to Tarot, as they say. Philippa should be willing to meet you halfway. She can't just swan in here and expect to change things."

"That's not the point," Dana began, and then her head went up, and I knew her precog ability was acting up because she always looked like a dog with pricked-up ears (in a good way).

I didn't have to be precog to know exactly what was happening when the doorbell rang.

Philippa brought sugar cookies in the shapes of pentacles, and holly and ivy and oak leaves, evergreens, and suns and moons. Of course. She swept into the room, a big smile on her face.

"Dana, Maggie!" She saw me. Her smile faltered, although she gamely tried to paste it back on. "...oh, hello, Kimberly."

Philippa had deep blue eyes and tousled dark hair, into which she'd tucked the fascinator I'd made at Samhain, much to my surprise. It was in her color, midnight blue, with a little scrap of a veil. She had that English peaches-and-cream complexion, and cheekbones that could slice glass. She wore a flowing black lace top, skinny jeans, and lace-up pointed-toe black Victorian boots. A little Helena Bonham Carter, a little Nigella Lawson.

I really hoped that low growl in the back of my throat was something I was just imagining. To be safe, I cleared my throat. "Hi, Philippa. It's good to see you." I even smiled.

Look, even I knew I was acting like an ass. I couldn't change the way I felt, but I had control over what I did despite my feelings. Maggie was probably right: we needed to meet halfway. So I stood, hugged Philippa hello. She smelled like violets, sweet and green, an unexpected scent in the darkening days of winter.

We re-seated ourselves.

"Did you bring any presents to wrap?" Dana asked Philippa.

"Oh, I'm afraid not," Philippa said, and I felt an unGoddess-like twinge of satisfaction before she added, "I've been making paper for two days, and it's not quite ready for wrapping yet."

"You're making your own wrapping paper?" Maggie

said. "Wow! Maybe you can do a demo at the school after the holidays."

Hey. I thought Maggie was on *my* side.

Next year, clearly, I was going to have to weave my own cloth to make gift bags.

"Before I forget," I said, even though I hadn't forgotten, but I wanted to make my change of subject seem natural, "has everyone decided what they're bringing to the dessert exchange?"

One of our holiday traditions was a party where everyone brought cookies and other holiday desserts—individual mince pies, pecan squares, brownies, that sort of thing. We sampled and drank wassail and eggnog, and at the end of the evening, everyone went home with an assortment of desserts.

"You're doing your peppermint fudge again, right?" Dana asked.

I shook my head. I had to go for *spectacular* this year. I was thinking about peppermint ice cream bonbons that stayed frozen on their own. I didn't tell them because I wanted it to be a surprise. "I'm branching out."

"Nooooo!" Maggie said. "I love your fudge. It's the best part of Yule!"

"My kids will slay me if I don't come home with it," Dana agreed. "And Georgine is probably going to faint dead away." Our friend Georgine *was* rather dramatic, it was true.

"You will all survive," I said, secretly pleased. Handed down through generations of my family, my peppermint fudge had a secret ingredient that added both taste and magic.

"Hmm..." said Philippa. "I don't suppose there's a list of

what everyone's bringing, so we don't all bring the same thing."

"Afraid not," I said, catching myself before I said something about how we all knew because we'd been doing this for years. It really wasn't her fault she was new. It was just her attitude. I could see those wheels turning.

"I think these cookies are wonderful," Dana said, waving one of the pentacle sugar cookies. "Or you could bring something that's been your tradition in the past. Even if it's similar to someone else's, you'll have put your own spin on it."

I actually felt calmer than I had in awhile. My dessert would be the most impressive, I'd get my reputation back, and Philippa would learn to meet me halfway.

It was the perfect plan.

If only I'd had Dana's precog abilities...

THE ANNUAL SOLSTICE dessert exchange was held at my house, largely because my great-grandmother had started the tradition in the neighborhood.

The dark wood paneled wainscoting gleamed under the glow of candles, which I had magically hung in midair above our heads, not close enough to the high ceiling to scorch. (What can I say? I was inspired by *Harry Potter*.) Evergreen garland wove between the white candles in a Celtic knotwork pattern and cast a pine scent throughout the house.

This was my favorite time of year—not the Solstice per se, but the gathering of families. My fellow witch-sisters, their partners, their children and parents. I had differently decorated trees set up in various rooms (one pagan, one colorful, one white and silver and purple, one random childhood decorations), a full bar as well as wassail warming of its own accord, and games for the children in the playroom. Oh, and the Playstation in the media room for the older kids and the young at heart.

The heavy dining room table of black walnut was covered with my great-grandmother's linen tablecloth and antique tiered serving platters, on which I'd placed white china plates with a delicate holly border and gilded edges. As attendees arrived, they arranged their desserts on the plates. In the kitchen, for later, I had holiday Tupperware for the exchange, decorated with each family's name in calligraphy.

Philippa and her husband, Cecil, arrived. He was blond to her dark, with a solid sort of Rex Harrison thing going on. She was in red, which highlighted her coloring, and she seemed...sort of excited, which was outside of her usual realm of cool and reservedly British.

A moment before I saw Philippa's dessert offering, Dana was suddenly at my side, Maggie a moment behind her. Uh oh. What had Dana *seen*?

And then I saw what Philippa had brought for the exchange.

Peppermint fudge.

Sweet chocolate and spicy peppermint wafted into my senses, followed by...no. It couldn't be.

Calling energy up from the earth and down from the moon, I squinted at the squares, so prettily decorated with shavings of red, green, and white peppermint flakes, but my sight went past that, into the fudge, into the very ingredients and their proportions. (I told you it was my thing.)

And then I saw it, oh yes I did.

The secret ingredient. Just a hint of candied ginger,

which in our tradition speaks of heat, added to keep the eater warm while the sun returns.

My head snapped up. "You stole my recipe?"

Everyone stopped talking. The room got very, very quiet, except for Blackmore's Night's "Mid Winter's Night" singing through the hidden speakers my husband, Eric, had installed.

Philippa's eyes grew larger, if such a thing were even possible. "No, I...I borrowed it. Everyone was saying how much they'd miss your fudge because you weren't making it, so I thought... I didn't think you'd mind..."

"That was a secret recipe handed down through my family," I said. "Guarded, prized. And you..."

Philippa shook her head, color blooming in her pale cheeks. "I had no idea," she whispered. "I just thought people would enjoy it."

Everyone was watching us. I tamped back my anger. Even the question of *how* was suddenly obvious to me. I'd hosted the Solstice ritual planning meeting a few days ago, all thirteen of us. She hadn't been alone in the kitchen, but it wouldn't have been hard, when no one was looking, to flick a hand and raise the card out of my recipe box long enough to commit the recipe to memory.

"You'll forget what you learned," I said. It wouldn't've taken much to add magic to my words, ensure that what I said came to pass. But in front of everyone, I had to make it Philippa's choice—plus I would never, ever tamper with someone's memory.

Philippa bowed her head. "So mote it be," she murmured.

Everyone breathed out. She'd sworn to forget it; the crisis was over.

Still, I entertained the charming fantasy of making an

unholy screeching noise and launching myself across the table, scattering sugary delicacies everywhere, to tackle her.

"Thank you," I said.

Dana's head swung towards the foyer moments before the doorbell rang. The person nearest to the front door opened it, and we heard a chorus of voices.

Ah, the carolers. Every year they came, stubbornly singing their Christian songs. We respected their beliefs—and their tenacity—and were very good about not sniggering if they sang "The Holly and the Ivy," because we knew what it was really about.

I lagged behind as everyone trooped to the door. As soon as the last person was around the corner out of the dining room, I waved a hand over Philippa's fudge and softly spoke a few choice words.

I would never have done anything to Philippa's dessert had she not stolen my secret recipe. It would have been hitting below the broomstick. I wanted to best her fair and square, not by being manipulative with magic. I had *standards*.

I'd meant only to make the fudge taste bad, have a gritty texture, to make people think that even with a simple, tried-and-true recipe, Philippa still couldn't pull it off.

But when everyone trooped back from the carolers and gathered around the table overflowing with desserts, a lot of people reached for the fudge. Let's face it, controversy is sexy. They wanted to find out if Philippa's fudge was as good as mine.

Everyone who sampled the fudge got an...unusual expression on their faces.

It was all I could do to keep from smiling.

But then, one by one, they reached into their mouths and pulled out a small origami crane.

Both Philippa and I flushed. At least, I assumed I did, given the rising heat I felt.

In Celtic mythology, cranes symbolized envy.

Dammit. I *knew* better than to try to cast a spell after a couple of glasses of Pinot Grigio.

Half the partygoers looked at me with pity, and the other half looked at Philippa with the same expression.

Well. That was interesting. At least fifty percent of my friends were on my side. That's what the looks meant, right?

The dessert exchange broke up soon after that. Apparently a good number of people didn't trust *any* of the treats after the crane incident, because I was left with a mountain of cookies. I was able to persuade Maggie to take most of them to school: "At the end of the day I'll sugar up the little bastards and send them home," she said with more glee than she ought to have had.

Dana, who had children in the school, closed her eyes and muttered a string of impressive obscenities.

I didn't blame her. I didn't need precog ability to know we should all be bracing ourselves.

THE NIGHT of the Solstice was bright and clear, with that blue-black sky that only a winter's night can bring. The snow glittered beneath the dome of sparkling stars. Earth and air, water and fire.

We celebrate our rituals in the park in the center of the neighborhood. The snow was soft underfoot as we crossed the green, and of course our footsteps disappeared as we went. It wasn't brutally cold, although the whole idea of doing a ritual skyclad was clearly made up by people who lived in warmer climates.

So we wore warm boots, thick stockings, heavy skirts and sweaters. Instead of hats, wreaths of holly adorned everyone's heads except for mine and Philippa's, to be burned in the bonfire during the ritual. (Yes, we have a firepit in the middle of our park for ritual purposes. We also have a turf labyrinth, and a communal garden for magical herbs.)

The fire lit, we joined hands in a circle. Thirteen of us, singing praise to the Goddess and the God, our voices rising through the air, visible thanks to the cold. Drawing up energy from the earth and down from the moon.

And so we raised a Circle, invisible to the untrained eye, domed over our heads and beneath our feet. A sacred place.

We dropped hands.

Last night, we'd met, all thirteen of us, and drawn Tarot cards from a deck that couldn't be influenced by magic. A truly random drawing, to see which two witches would lead the ritual this year.

The powers that be showed their sense of humor. Of *course* Philippa and I drew the most powerful cards: the Empress and the High Priestess.

"I'll follow your lead," Philippa had said, and I'd said "I'll email you the plan," which I had. It wasn't much different from past rituals, but she'd extended her olive branch, and I'd extended mine.

Now, she and I stepped to the center of the circle, on one side of the fire, the other women closing the gaps behind us.

Even a few steps closer to the fire changed the temperature. Whew. My body tingled from the combined energy of earth, air, fire, water, and spirit. I felt calm, centered.

Between us was the altar, solid and heavy, carved from an enormous walnut stump generations ago. We each lit a fat white pillar candle, one ringed with holly, the other with oak leaves. Then we each picked up the wreaths. I settled holly on my head; Philippa nestled oak on hers.

I breathed in the crisp snowy air, tasted the smoky scent of the fire. It was exhilarating.

"Now is the time of the winter solstice, the time of darkest night," I said. "The time of the Holly King."

"Yet now, it is also the time of His death," Philippa intoned, "so that he may be reborn at the lightest time of summer."

With each phrase, I felt the energy pulse and grow. But it felt, too, as if we were pushing at each other, even though we weren't physically touching. We should have been sharing, mingling our energies.

"This is a celebration of rebirth," I said. "The Holly King lays down his mantle..."

"...and the Oak King reclaims his," Philippa said.

"The Holly King passes..."

"...and the Oak King is born of the Goddess."

Even though I'd written the bulk of the ritual, when I'd emailed it to Philippa, I'd said I was open to suggestions, and she'd given me some, and I had included them. But now, every time Philippa spoke, I felt as though she was challenging my words, trying to make hers better, stronger. As much as I tried to tamp it down, my annoyance with her grew with every passing moment.

We said the next sentences, but instead of combining our energy, agreeing, speaking as one, I felt her drawing up more energy and shoving it at me.

"As the Wheel turns, the old king's strength wanes as a new challenger rises to claim the hand of the Goddess," I said. But I was thinking *No. You don't have more power than me.* I matched her, held my ground, imagining a shield. "The kings of Holly and Oak, of waning and waxing, of dark and light, must do battle on this day."

Philippa's eyes glittered dark in the firelight. She almost sounded sarcastic as she said, "I crown the Holly King, lord of the waning year. Now is the time of your greatest power. Are you ready to do battle for the hand of our Goddess?"

I thought I heard Maggie's voice, so very faint in my head, saying *Kimberly...*, her tone a plea, a warning. I thought I felt something from Dana, which in words would translate approximately to *Oh shitballs.*

If I backed down, Philippa would overwhelm me. The ritual was about balance, and I had to stand my ground, defend myself.

"I crown the Oak King, lord of the waxing year," I said. "Your season is almost upon us. Are you ready to do battle for the hand of our Goddess?"

I spoke the question as an answer to hers: *hell yeah, bring it on.*

In some traditions, people act out the choreographed battle between the two aspects of the God; in others, they reenact the birth of the new God from the loins of the Goddess. We simply raised our hands, closed our eyes, imagined the battle between the Gods and the resurrection of the Oak King.

As one, we knew the moment when the world poised in the very middle of the longest night of the year, about to tip toward the light again.

One by one, going deosil, or sunwise, around the circle, all thirteen of us tossed our circlets into the fire. The holly was subsumed by the flames from the oak logs, symbolizing the Holly King's darkness submitting to the Oak King's light.

Or, at least, it was supposed to.

Instead, I threw my holly wreath in, the final symbol of the dying Holly King, then Philippa threw in her oak leaf wreath, a symbol of the Oak King triumphing in his blaze of glory...

...but the fire *went out*.

I blinked in the sudden darkness, feeling as if I was coming out of a trance. My sight adjusted to the dim light provided by the candles and the stars and the faint reflection off the snow, but my eyes watered from the smoke billowing from the firepit.

"Uh oh," I said. "That wasn't supposed to happen." I looked at Philippa. Her eyes no longer looked as black, but they were wide with guilt. "What did you do?" I demanded.

"Me?" She reared back. "I didn't bloody do anything. What did *you* do?"

You moved here. But I didn't say it. Instead I took a long, deep breath in, blew it out and watched the air swirl in the cold. "It doesn't matter now. Now we have to fix things." I looked beyond her at the semicircle of women staring at us, then turned around to look at the semicircle behind us.

But they weren't staring at us. None of them were. They were all staring through the trees, down the street. Dana was muttering an impressively blistering string of curses.

I followed their gaze, and felt my stomach drop. Behind me, Philippa gasped.

They were all looking at my house.

My house, with my wonderful rooftop decoration of life-sized Holly and Oak kings battling it out.

Only now they weren't decorations, and they really *were* battling.

Where in Annwn had they gotten *swords*? I hadn't given the figures swords. They were my *holiday decorations*.

Holiday decorations who were going to do some serious damage to my wrought iron widow's walk if they kept this up.

"Okay," I said, raising my voice enough that everyone finally turned to look at me. "Let's figure out how to fix this. Together we can—"

"Oh, no," Dana said, as she and Maggie and the rest of the coven all took a collective step backwards. "This is all on you and Philippa. We had nothing to do with it."

Panic fluttered in my stomach. "No, we were all doing the ritual," I protested, even though I had a growing terror that they were right.

"The bulk of the energy was coming from the two of you," Maggie said.

"And the God took over your decorations," Dana pointed out.

They stepped closer to Philippa and I, and Dana added, quietly, so the rest of the coven couldn't hear, "Look, this happened because the two of you were having a pissing match instead of honoring the ritual. You two need to work it out on your own, between the two of you."

"I don't think there's anything the rest of us can do to help," Maggie added, sotto voce.

"But call us if you need us," Dana added.

Before Philippa or I could protest, they stepped back into the circle of women.

Around us, everyone clasped hands and raised them to the heavens, then slowly brought them down, finally crouching to release and splay their fingers on the snow, releasing the Circle, returning the energy.

I automatically did the same, as did Philippa. Unreleased energy was headache-inducing at best, dangerous at worst. Still, I was a little miffed that they all dropped the Circle without discussing it with us.

But I also knew Dana and Maggie were right. Philippa and I had done this.

We had to be the ones to fix it.

"Right," I said, pulling my gloves back on, "let's go reclaim the balance and bring back the light."

I wished I felt half as confident as I sounded.

I stomped back out of the village green, Philippa double-timing to catch up. We didn't bother to erase our steps in the snow.

When Philippa caught up to me, she said, "I think the Tarot choosing us to perform the ritual together was a sign."

"You think?" I snapped, then shook my head, swallowing my anger. In a milder tone, I said, "Yes, you're right. There are no coincidences."

"Any theories about why?" she asked.

Well, at least it was nice to be asked, instead of challenged. I no longer felt her energy pushing at me; now, though, it was more of a wall she'd retreated behind. Or maybe a shield. I didn't take much satisfaction in the thought that maybe she was scared of what I might do. A teensy-tiny bit of satisfaction, maybe, because hey, I'm only human, right?

"Not yet," I admitted.

That iota of smugness vanished as we got closer to my house.

I'd made life-sized figures of the two aspects of the God. Now they were...well, maybe life-sized for *them*.

They were huge.

The widow's walk at the top of my house had a wrought-iron railing that hit a little above waist height; probably would've hit Philippa at the waist, given that she's a bit taller than me.

It came to the Gods' knees.

I didn't think there was any way to go up there without being squished or flung off or otherwise suffering some unhappy bodily injury. It wasn't so much that the Gods would turn on us, but that right now, we weren't in their realm of consciousness. Their battle was their battle.

Which was how it always was. We invite the spirits to enter our Circle, join us in our ritual and celebration, but it's not as if they're partying with us on their level.

They're on a whole 'nother level altogether.

"Hey!" I yelled anyway. "*Hey! Knock it off!*"

Philippa stared at me. "Bloody hell," she said, her breath curling around her face. "You're going to get us both killed. You can't speak to them that way!"

"I'm just trying to get their attention," I said.

"And *then* what?" she demanded. "Ask them nicely to settle their differences and shake hands and oh, let one defeat the other because it would be lovely to see the sun rise?"

"Do you have a better plan?" I asked.

She pursed those lush lips together and glanced away. Finally she said, "Not yet. I'm just trying to say that perhaps mortal solutions are less likely to work."

"Because using magic to make things easier is *always* the solution." It came out before I could stop it. It held all of the frustration and anger and, yes, fear that had been caroming inside of me since she showed up, magnified by this much, much bigger problem raging over our heads.

She took a step back as if I'd slapped her, and I felt like an ass.

"I'm sorry," I said, knowing the words were lame. I forced the next words out; I didn't want to say them, but they were true. "We shouldn't be fighting about our problems, because that—" I pointed up, even though neither of us had to look "—needs to be our focus. Let's...let's take a minute to ground and center, then look at our options. No idea gets shot down without consideration."

Her chin went up; her mouth was in a tight line. In the near-darkness, her eyes still seemed huge. Finally, she gave a curt nod. "Very well. Because if we can't figure this out, the sun isn't going to rise."

She tilted her head to the east, and I realized with horror that she was right. By this time, it should have been growing lighter, the black into gray, soon to be the pale pink of deep winter dawn.

There was nothing but the blue-blackness of eternal midnight.

This wasn't about the two of us—this was about bringing back the light for the whole world.

I stared up at the kings of summer and winter, of dark and light, wrestling on the roof of my house. The Oak King seemed to be more of the aggressor; the Holly King, the defender.

I closed my eyes. Drew in a long breath, connected with the energy of earth and sky, just enough to clear my mind and emotions so I could really meditate on the problem. The sounds on the roof—the grunts, the thuds, the twang of wrought iron that was probably going to snap and rain down and impale us—faded.

Lord and Lady, help me see clearly, I thought, and a moment later, clarity slammed upside my head in a cosmic two-by-four of obviousness.

Ow. But I sent a *thank you* into the universe and faced what should have been evident from the start, if only I'd been open enough to see it.

I was like the Holly King, fighting to keep things the same, and Philippa represented the newness of the Oak King. I resisted the transition, the change, because I felt threatened, rather than being open to the knowledge that the Wheel always must turn.

I opened my eyes, turned to Philippa. Because we were half-between the worlds, I saw that oak wreath on her head again, and didn't have to reach up to feel the prick of holly leaves to know my own wreath was there.

"Dana was right," I said. "We did cause this. *I* caused this. I've been jealous of you ever since you moved here, because you represented change, and I wanted things to stay the same. Instead of infusing the energy of transition into the ritual, I resisted—just like the Holly King is doing. And the harder you pushed, the harder I fought back."

"Kimberly," Philippa said urgently, "I respect your standing in the community. I don't want to take over. I just want to share...and learn from you, too."

"Me? What are you talking about?"

"You're right," she said quietly. "I'm not good at many things, and I've always fallen back on magic. But you, you're perfect. Everything you do is at a level I can't even imagine. You *are* magic."

I just...I don't...

"And I've gone about things the wrong way; I see that now," she added. "Of course you felt threatened by me, the way I was acting. I thought I was being neighborly, participating in the potlucks and baking for everyone. But I was using that as an excuse, when really, I wanted people to like me as much as they like you."

Fuck. I wasn't going to say it to Philippa, but maybe I *did* feel like my standing the community was lodged in what I could provide, rather than who I was.

"We're idiots," I said, which provoked a startled laugh from her.

"I do believe we are," she agreed.

"As much as I hate to admit it, this isn't a time for doing things the hard way," I said. "This *is* a time for magic."

We joined hands, and repeated the words of the ritual. It was the time of the Holly King, and the time of his death, and the time of the rebirth of the Holly King into the Oak King, who would bring back the light and lead us towards summer. This time, we didn't oppose with our words or our energies; we spoke together, and the energy flowed back and forth, open.

At the Summer Solstice, the Oak King would step down and make way for the Holly King to return. An eternal cycle.

And all the while, the Goddess watches over all.

For a brief moment, Philippa and I were Goddess, mourning the Holly King while celebrating the Oak King's birth.

The sounds of battle above us faded.

"Look," Philippa whispered.

I opened my eyes.

In the east, the faint tendrils of dawn.

I let out a breath I hadn't realized I'd been holding, relief making me weak-limbed. We dropped hands, released the energy, fingers buried in the snow.

"Well," she said, rising to her feet and brushing off her

brown leather gloves, "I'm knackered, and Cecil must be wondering why the ritual's taking so long."

"You two want to come over for dinner tonight?" I asked.

She smiled. "We'd love to—if you'll come over next week."

"Just no peppermint fudge," I said.

She nodded. "Actually, I'd love it if you could teach me to bake. When I try to do it on my own, things burn, collapse, or explode."

"I'll put up a protective shield," I said.

She turned and started to walk away. I almost headed into my house, but instead, I crouched down, scooped up some snow, and nailed her in the middle of the back with a snowball.

With a shriek, she turned, and a moment later I tried to duck one coming at me, but she probably had put just a weak bit of magic in it, because it landed on my forehead, spattering my face with icy cold flakes.

I had no clue where the rest of the coven had been hiding, but the next thing we knew, they were all there, and it was some sort of crazy free-for-all. Even fastidious, dramatic Georgine.

I couldn't remember the last time I'd laughed so hard.

Things were only going to get better. I didn't need Dana's precog abilities to tell me that.

I was going to make things better.

BE THE FIRST TO KNOW!

Sign up for Dayle A. Dermatis's newsletter for *free* fiction, plus the latest news, releases, and more.

Sign up at DayleDermatis.com.

For more in-depth conversations and special sneak peeks, you can also support her continued work by joining her community of patrons out Dayle's Patreon.

Patreon.com/Dayle

About the Author

Dayle A. Dermatis is the author or coauthor of many novels (including snarky urban fantasies *Ghosted* and the forthcoming *Shaded* and *Spectered*) and more than a hundred short stories in multiple genres, appearing in such venues as *Fiction River*, *Alfred Hitchcock's Mystery Magazine*, and DAW Books.

Called the mastermind behind the *Uncollected Anthology* project, she also guest edits anthologies for *Fiction River*, and her own short fiction has been lauded in many year's best anthologies in erotica, mystery, and horror.

She lives in a historic English-style cottage with a tangled and fae back garden, in the wild greenscapes of the Pacific Northwest. In her spare time she follows Styx around the country and travels the world, which inspires her writing.

She'd love to have you over for a virtual cup of tea or glass of wine at DayleDermatis.com, where you can also sign up for her newsletter and support her on Patreon.

~

I value honest feedback, and would love to hear your opinion in a review, if you're so inclined, on your favorite book retailer's site.

~

For more information:
www.dayledermatis.com

ALSO BY DAYLE A. DERMATIS

NOVELS

The Nikki Ashburne Novels

Ghosted

Shaded (forthcoming)

Spectered (forthcoming)

Beautiful Beast

Waking the Witch

What Beck'ning Ghost

COLLECTIONS

Devilish Deals and Perilous Pacts: A Spooky Collection of Deals With the Devil and Other Bad Choices

Five Funny Fantasies

Haunted (a Nikki Ashburne collection, forthcoming)

Powerful Girls: A YA Short Story Collection

Small Wonders: Ten Short-Short Speculative Fiction Stories

Umberto Scolari and the Five Mysteries: A Short Story Collection

Voices Carry and Other Stories of Women and Crime

Written on the Coast: Thirteen Stories of Magic and Mayhem Written in Lincoln City, OR

NONFICTION

*Researching History for Fantasy Writers: How to Use Historical Detail
to Make Your Fantasy Worlds Rich and Compelling*

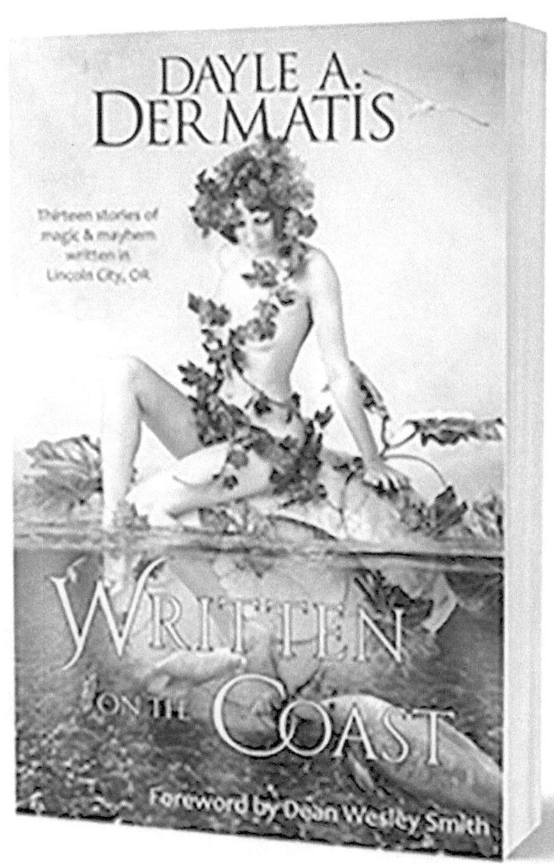

DAYLE A. DERMATIS
Thirteen stories of magic & mayhem written in Lincoln City, OR
WRITTEN ON THE COAST
Foreword by Dean Wesley Smith

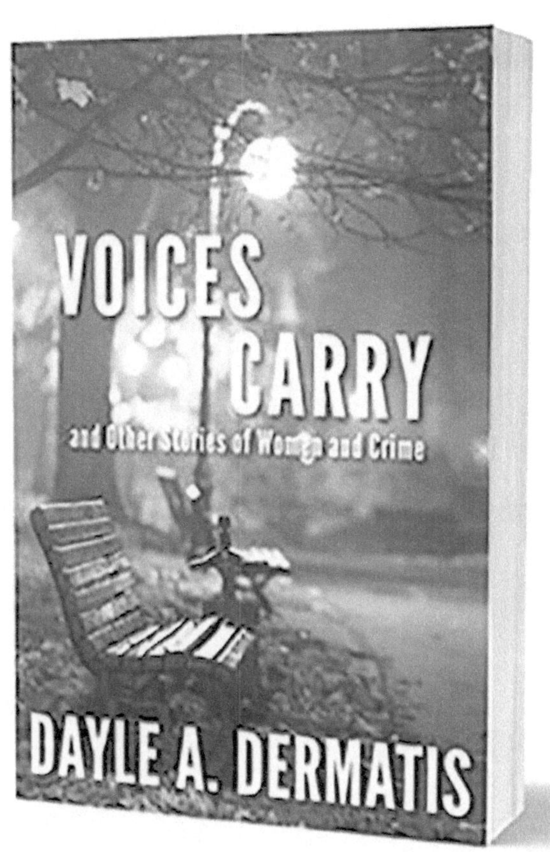

VOICES
CARRY
and Other Stories of Women and Crime
DAYLE A. DERMATIS

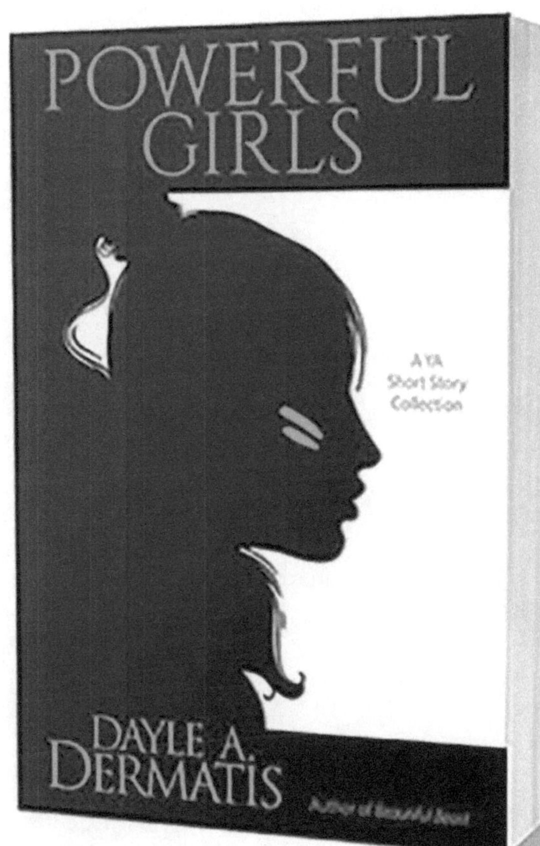
POWERFUL
GIRLS
A YA
Short Story
Collection
DAYLE A.
DERMATIS
Author of Beautiful Secret